# OUR

The girls waved as Sasha descended the steps and turned down the street.

"Ok," said Faye to Melanie, putting her hands on her hips. "What was that about? Why did you stop me mentioning the code? She might have had some ideas for us."

"I don't know," said Melanie. "It just feels like it should be a secret." She started walking distractedly down the front steps. "It's like what we were talking about earlier. Mardi Gras is full of secrets. Why shouldn't we have one, too?"

"But we've already asked people for help," said Faye.

"Yeah," said Kate. "I got Mr. Simmington's name from my parents. And Sasha told us which parades he designs."

"Those are just clues," said Melanie. "Coming straight out and telling people about the code wouldn't feel the same. This is our puzzle. Just ours." She looked at her friends. "Can't we at least try? Just us?"

Kate smiled, and Faye nodded.

"Just us," agreed Faye.

"Our own Mardi Gras mystery," said Kate.

Melanie grabbed them both in a quick impulsive hug. "Exactly," she said. "And you know what?" She pulled back and smiled with suppressed excitement. "I think we just might solve it, too."

# The Mardi Gras Chase

OTHER WORKS BY MAGGIE M. LARCHE

Striker Jones: Elementary Economics for
Elementary Detectives

Striker Jones and the Midnight Archer

Charlie Bingham Gets Clocked

Charlie Bingham Gets Serious

# The Mardi Gras Chase

MAGGIE M. LARCHE

Leopold Press

This is a work of fiction and, as such, it is a product of the author's creative imagination. All names of characters appearing in these pages are fictitious. Any similarities of characters to real persons, whether living or dead, are coincidental. Any resemblance of incidents portrayed in this book to actual events, other than public events, is likewise coincidental.

Publisher's Cataloging-In-Publication Data
(Prepared by The Donohue Group, Inc.)


Larche, Maggie M.
  The Mardi Gras chase / Maggie M. Larche.

    pages ;  cm. -- ([True girls] ; [1])

  Summary: "Twelve-year-old Melanie is bored with her little sister and with yet another Mardi Gras in her hometown. But when she notices a secret code built into the floats of a Mardi Gras parade, she realizes that life might have some surprises left. Melanie and her friends set off to break the Mardi Gras code. They chase clues throughout the season's parades, sneak into forbidden float barns, and even join forces with the intriguing boy who lives down the street. When they uncover the final clue, Melanie must decide how much she's willing to risk to learn the secret of the Mardi Gras code."--Provided by publisher.
  Series statement supplied by publisher.
  Interest age level: 007-012.
  ISBN: 978-0-692-54866-0

  1. Carnival--Juvenile fiction. 2. Parades--Juvenile fiction.
3. Ciphers--Juvenile fiction. 4. Preteens--Juvenile fiction. 5. Mardi
Gras--Fiction. 6. Parades--Fiction. 7. Ciphers--Fiction. 8. Preteens--Fiction.
9. Mystery and detective stories. I. Title.

PZ7.L27 Ma 2015
[Fic]

# 1

The downtown street exploded in color, with bright greens, reds, and purples sparkling under tinsel and glitter. Jazz music and drumlines competed with the yelling spectators to vibrate the air with sound. Cheap treasures rained down on the crowds, and coins sparkled as they clattered onto the pavement. It was wonderful, tumultuous chaos. And Melanie Smythurst was bored.

"Ugh," she said. "Let's go, guys. Please."

"Don't be such a grump," said her friend Kate Butler. "This is a great parade." She jumped with perfect timing and snagged a handful of purple beads out of the air. "Got it!"

"Seriously," said Faye Ryan. "You are being a downer, Mel." Faye frowned as Kate stuffed the beads into the pillowcase she carried. "And this parade would be *perfect* if Kate would stop hogging the throws. I've got to stop standing beside you. You are just too tall." She lifted her own limp pillowcase and compared it to Kate's, already half full. "This is pathetic."

"I'll buy you both a pile of beads if we head home now," said Melanie. Her red hair glowed from the spotlights of the passing float. "Loads of them. I promise."

"Nope," said Kate. "It's not the same. They have to be earned."

The girls were watching one of the many Mardi Gras parades in Mobile, Alabama. Lasting several weeks, Mobile's Mardi Gras was something most kids would envy – nightly parades, dazzling floats, free treats, days off from school, and the promise of balls to attend once they were older. It was a season of celebration for the city's residents.

"Besides," said Kate, "you know why we have to stay."

"Community pride," said Faye, keeping her eyes on the parade.

"Booty-dancing bands," said Kate.

Melanie crossed her arms. "Crowds and smells and –"

"Moon pies!" Kate interrupted as she caught one from the air. "Thank you!" she yelled to the masked marshal riding on horseback.

Melanie sighed and reached over Kate's shoulder. She plucked the sweet from her hand. "Ok, fine. I might stay for the moon pies." She peeled open the wrapper and took a bite.

"Mmm, peanut butter," she said with her mouth full.

"Gross," said Faye, while Kate just laughed.

"Well, look alive girls," said Melanie, stepping back again. "If we're staying, you might as well catch me some snacks."

Kate and Faye took positions on the barricade and prepared for the next round of throws.

"Come on," Kate said over her shoulder to Melanie, but Melanie wasn't listening.

Every float in the parade was preceded by a sign carrier, someone who walked on foot and displayed a placard that announced the theme of the upcoming float. The sign carrier for the float about to pass the girls was a hunched old man whose sign read, "Under the Sea." In spite of his age, the man strutted along with a grin on his face, bopping his head to the lively cadence blasting from a nearby marching band. The sign was tilted back on his shoulder.

"Look at the title," said Melanie, pointing to the man's sign. "The R in 'Under' is upside-down."

"What?" said Kate.

"I said, " Melanie broke off and raised her voice to be heard over the yells now coming from the crowd. "Look at the title."

"Whoohoo!" yelled Kate. She waved her hands in the air as the float passed.

The opulent structure was decorated with clownfish, mermaids, and the occasional octopus. Masked men wearing blue satin costumes stood among artificial waves cresting over their heads, throwing to the crowd below. One rider took a liking to Faye and Kate and showered them with beads and silk roses. The crowd pressed in on all sides to grab the throws that fell to the ground. They picked the ground clean in under five seconds.

After the float moved on, Kate turned again to Melanie.

"Sorry, Mel, what did you say?"

"Never mind," said Melanie. "I just noticed that one of the letters was upside-down on the sign for the float."

"That's weird," said Faye. "Shouldn't they catch that sort of thing beforehand?"

"Sounds to me," said Kate, "like the float builders started the party a little early, you know what I mean?"

Melanie took another bite of moon pie. A few new spectators arrived and sidled next to the girls. It was a family of five. The father carried the littlest boy wrapped up against the cold in a fleece bodysuit shaped like a bear. Melanie guessed him to be about two.

"Good luck catching anything now," she whispered to Faye and Kate. "We've got a baby."

"Darn it," said Kate quietly, glancing back over her shoulder. "Cute babies get all the throws."

"Ha," said Faye, the lights reflecting off her dark skin. "Now you can live like me and Mel for a while."

Melanie laughed and stepped back, enjoying her snack and the starry night filled with music. Though she wasn't crazy about Mardi Gras, she did enjoy a cold winter evening, an all-too-rare occurrence in Mobile.

She sighed and turned her attention back to the parade.

"Look," she said, pointing. "There's another one."

The sign for the next float came along, and right in the middle of the title – "Off to the Races" – was a backwards C.

"That's so strange," said Faye. "Maybe it's on purpose."

For the rest of the parade, Melanie searched for strange letters. The next sign was free from anything unusual, but the float itself hid a backwards E amongst the decorations.

She pulled out her phone and began documenting each letter she saw.

"What are you doing?" asked Kate.

Melanie looked up. "I'm writing the letters down. What if it's a sort of message? Like when movie credits spell out something for the audience who stays to the very end."

"I wouldn't think you'd care about a message if it came from Mardi Gras," said Faye.

"Well, it probably does say something stupid, like 'Come to Walmart for all your Mardi Gras needs,'" said Melanie. "But what else do I have to do?" But by the end of the parade, all Melanie had to show to Faye and Kate was a string of nonsensical letters.

"R, C, E, N, R, A, P," read Kate. She nodded

seriously. "Ah, yes, now it is all clear."

Faye laughed.

"Ok, so that was a waste," said Melanie. She locked her phone and dropped it into her pocket. "Even the Walmart ad would have been more interesting."

"You should have tried to catch stuff," said Kate. She lifted her pillowcase, now overflowing with beads of all colors. A little purple teddy bear stuck its head out of the top.

"Pretty good, huh?" She paused waiting for a reply. Rather than answering, Melanie and Faye just stared over her shoulder.

"What?" Kate asked, and Faye silently pointed behind her with a grin.

Kate turned to see the little boy in the fleece bear suit looking down from his perch on his father's shoulders. His father chatted with the rest of the family while the child gazed longingly at Kate's teddy bear.

"Oh, ok," Kate said, rolling her eyes. "Here you go." She handed the bear to the boy, who let out a shriek of delight.

Kate turned back to her friends. "Let's get out of here before I get hit up by more kids."

The bike ride back to their houses was eventful, what with the full bag that Kate had to carry somehow as she rode. Her bike lurched from side to side like a sleepy camel, and the girls were obliged to stop several times so Kate could reposition the bag of throws. By the time they made it to their street, they were all giggling uncontrollably.

"See you guys tomorrow," shouted Melanie, laughing as she pedaled slightly farther down the street from her two friends.

"Meet at my house," Faye's voice followed her.

Melanie waved her hand over her head to show she heard before coasting into her driveway. The house shined brightly in the night. Her stomach rumbled as she threw her bike into the garage and headed inside.

"Hey, sweetie," said her mother as Melanie walked into the kitchen. Mrs. Smythurst was a short, pleasant woman with vivid red hair. "How was the parade?"

Melanie shrugged and snatched a cherry tomato from a large salad bowl that her mother was clearing from the table. "Fine, I guess," she said, popping it into her mouth. "We had fun and all, but, you know... Same old, same old."

Her mom gave an understanding smile. "Were the floats any good?"

Melanie shrugged again. "Not bad. Kate caught a lot of stuff."

"That girl always does," said her mother with a laugh. She looked at Melanie's empty hands. "You didn't catch anything?"

Melanie shook her head. "What's the point? It's all just junk."

"Sweetie, if you don't enjoy the parade, why do you go?"

"I don't know. Habit?"

"Well, I know that feeling. Here, help yourself to spaghetti. Your dad's already putting Lacey to bed."

"Thanks, Mom." Melanie loaded up a plate with food and headed down the hall to her bedroom.

She sat down at her desk with her plate. She toyed with the noodles, lost in thought. She knew she'd fill the evening the way she always did. Lose herself in a book for a little while. Do the dishes. Get ready for bed. Rinse. Repeat.

Looking back, Melanie tried to pinpoint the moment when all this grey sameness took over her life, but couldn't. It snuck up on her, until one day, life didn't feel very exciting anymore.

At bedtime, Melanie committed one small act of rebellion against her dreary day-to-day routine. She skipped brushing her teeth before slipping into bed.

She relaxed into her mattress and ran her tongue over her fuzzy teeth. It was only a small gesture, but it was a step.

Two hours later, Melanie lay in bed, still unable to fall asleep. Feeling guilty over her uncompleted nightly routine, she finally pulled her phone off her bedside table to distract herself.

As the phone turned on, the light momentarily blinded her night-adjusted eyes. Squinting, she opened her note from earlier that evening.

"R, C, E, N, R, A, P."

Maybe it meant absolutely nothing. It probably meant absolutely nothing. But she couldn't help wondering.

"They might have hired a dyslexic painter," she said aloud. One of the boys in her class had dyslexia, and she knew he sometimes had trouble seeing the difference between "b" and "d" because he reversed the letters in his mind. But surely it wasn't the same person who both painted the signs and decorated the floats, was it?

"I'll just check one more thing," she muttered, "and then I am going to sleep. Hear that, world?" She spoke towards the ceiling. "I am going to sleep."

She pulled up the internet as she mentally reviewed what she knew about Mardi Gras. As the oldest Mardi Gras celebration in the country, Mobile's festivities were elaborate. Dozens of carnival organizations operated in the city, and many of them put on a parade sometime during the season. The groups used mystical names like Daughters of Time, the Hidden Branch, and Knights of Ra. Each one had its own floats, parade, ball, and unique style.

Melanie knew that the later you progressed in the season, the more parades, until finally, you reached Fat Tuesday, when the entire city slacked off work and spent the day celebrating.

That evening, Melanie and her friends had attended the parade by an organization called the Order of the Centaur, but other groups had already paraded that season.

Acting on some unnamed hunch, Melanie pulled up a parade schedule and searched for photos of the parade that ran the day before: Ancient Aztecs.

"No. No. No," she said as she clicked through

the pictures. "Ah ha!"

She stopped and stared at one picture – a sign carrier in the Aztecs parade. The sign read "Jumpin' Jack Flash."

"Backwards *F*," whispered Melanie to herself. "Gotcha."

Quickly, she searched for any online pictures she could find of all the previous parades. Even though five parades had already rolled that year, she couldn't find any other pictures of strange letters.

So at least two parades included the mysterious letters among the floats: the Centaurs and the Aztecs. And there were possibly more that weren't pictured. What did it mean? What tied them together?

"Whatever it is," said Melanie out loud to herself, "I'm going to figure it out."

She put her phone down and snuggled back under her covers. She didn't know what it all meant. She only knew that, finally, here was something different. And for now, maybe that was enough.

# 2

After breakfast on Saturday morning, Melanie pulled her hair back into a long ponytail down her back. When she turned twelve the previous month, she adopted the look as her signature hairstyle. Just having a signature hairstyle made her feel very sophisticated.

She pulled on her tennis shoes and laced them up as her younger sister popped her head in the door.

Even Melanie had to admit that Lacey was adorable. Only three years old, Lacey sported classic dimples and a blond bob haircut that tended to float around her head like a halo. Kate had previously considered using her at the parade as bait for more throws, but the girls scrapped that idea when they realized it would mean Melanie's parents would probably come, too.

"Hey," said Lacey, wandering into the room. "Whatcha doing? Are you leaving?"

"Yep. Sorry, Bug. I'm heading to Faye's."

"Can I go with you? I like Faye. She won't mind."

"Not today," said Melanie. "Why don't you go find Mom or Dad? They'll play with you."

"That's not fun," said Lacey. She wandered around Melanie's room and picked up a hairbrush from Melanie's dresser. She stood on her tiptoes to peer into the mirror. When she tried to brush her own hair, it simply made her hair stand even higher than it had moments before.

Melanie finished tying her sneakers and stood up briskly. She removed the brush from Lacey's hand and replaced it on the dresser. Then she scooted Lacey out the door in front of her, pulling the door closed behind her.

"Ok, now stay out of my room while I'm gone."

"But Mel," said Lacey.

"See ya!" Melanie ran down the hall, shouting "Mom, Dad, I'm out. Lacey's looking for you." She ran out the front door and down the street.

She quickly covered the three houses between hers and Faye's and knocked on the door loudly. Experience had taught her that Faye practiced her violin every Saturday morning, so she banged her fist to be heard above the music.

"Good morning, Melanie," said Faye's mother, a willowy woman with chocolaty skin. "She's upstairs. Just follow the racket." She flushed. "Music. I mean music."

Melanie hid her grin. "Thanks, Mrs. Ryan." Melanie headed up the stairs and walked straight into Faye's bedroom.

Faye stood in the middle of the room in front of a folding metal music stand. She was cranking out an unrecognizable piece of music on her violin. Melanie cringed.

"Oh, thank the Lord," said Faye, dropping the violin from her shoulder. "Now that you're here, I've got a good excuse to stop practicing."

"Rough way to start every weekend, hmm?" asked Melanie, plopping onto Faye's bed.

"You're telling me," said Faye, placing her instrument into its case. "The funny thing is, everyone knows I'm awful. Dad always finds an excuse to do yard work when I start up. And mom's always got a headache by the time I'm done." Faye sighed and slid the instrument and music stand below her bed. "But she keeps on insisting that it's going to look great on college applications, so I keep on playing."

"We've got years and years until then," said Melanie. "That's a long time to do something you hate."

"Tell that to my mom."

"Let the constant violin music wear her down. She'll crack eventually," said Melanie. "When's Kate getting here?"

"I dunno. Soon, I think. She said last night that she'd be over early." Kate's house was located just across the street from Faye's.

"Good," said Melanie, sitting up. Her eyes shone as she leaned forward. "Because I've got something to talk to you two about."

"Ooh," said Faye. "What is it?"

"Wait for Kate," said Melanie. "Besides, I think I hear her."

A distant pounding noise grew louder as someone bounded up the stairs, and the door flung open to reveal their friend.

"Hey, guys," Kate said and flopped onto the floor. She shook out her hair, still wet. "I was so glad to get out of my house this morning."

Faye laughed. "Trouble with the munchkins?"

"Yep," said Kate. "Little brothers two through four." Kate was one of six siblings and the only girl. She and her twin brother Matt were the oldest, and both of them consistently referred to the younger boys by their birth order, rather than name. With four younger siblings in the house, they maintained that it was easier to refer to them by number.

"First," continued Kate, stretching out her legs in front of her, "number four decided to build a catapult out of tinker toys. Then, boys two and three loaded that catapult with the blueberry oatmeal Mom made for breakfast."

Faye and Melanie groaned. Kate nodded.

"Uh huh. It was chaos. Absolute chaos. Mom and Dad were yelling. Boys were running and hiding. I had oatmeal in my hair and had to rewash it. And everywhere," she continued over Melanie and Faye's laughter, "there were these blobs of blueberry goo. The whole kitchen's blue. It's disgusting."

Kate leaned forward and touched her toes.

"I was lucky to get out of there," she said, her voice muffled from speaking into her knees. "I thought Mom would rope me into cleaning up the mess, but she finally made the boys clean up after themselves. She even made Matt join in."

"Why Matt?" asked Faye. "I thought it was the littles."

"Matt put them up to it. He always does." Kate sat straight up again. "So, I do not want to go home for a while. What should we do today instead?"

"I'm glad you asked," said Melanie. "I've got a project for us."

Faye smiled. "She's been waiting for you to dish."

"Ok," said Kate. "What's up?"

Melanie began by telling them about her research of the previous night. When she finished, Faye frowned.

"So you're saying that more than one parade has got these backwards letters? And what does that mean?" asked Faye.

"I don't know, exactly," said Melanie. "But I don't think it can be by accident. Remember last night when I said it might be a secret message? I've been thinking about it all night – what if it's a code? A code across parades?" She pulled out her phone. "R, C, E, N, R, A, P," she read again. "Makes no sense right? But, now we know there are *other* parades with these strange letters. So it doesn't make sense yet, but that's because we only have some of the clues."

"And you want us to…" said Kate.

"Find the rest of the letters and solve the code," said Melanie.

"Obviously," said Faye.

"Kind of sounds like a lot of work," said Kate.

"And a lot of parades," said Faye. She looked at Melanie. "Are you really suggesting we go to every single parade? There are tons left, and you hate them."

"I don't hate them."

"Come on, Mel," said Kate. "We know you do."

"Anyway," said Melanie, "I'm hoping it won't come to that. I've been thinking about how to go about this. I think we need to figure out why the code has been in some parades and not others. If we can do that, we might be able to tell which future parades we need to watch."

"I guess let's do it," said Kate after a pause. "I'm up for anything. Besides, it's got to be better than scraping oatmeal from the walls."

Melanie smiled. "Faye?"

"Well, it is kind of a busy week coming up. I've got to do well on our math test." She looked at the expression on Melanie's face and laughed. "But of course I'm in."

"Ok, good," said Melanie. "You scared me for a sec, Faye, but I knew I could count on you guys. I really think we're on to something."

"So, let's get started," said Faye, ever the organizer of the group. "Which other parades did you say the code has already been in?"

"Aztecs," said Melanie.

"And now the Centaurs, too," said Faye.

The girls opened Faye's laptop and pulled up what parade pictures they could find. They spent the next hour trying to find a connection between the two parades.

"Well, they both follow the same route," said Kate.

"So do all the parades," said Melanie.

Minutes later, Faye remarked, "They're both at night?"

"Good one," said Kate, and Melanie nodded. She wrote down on a sheet of paper: "Nighttime."

"They include marching bands?" said Kate.

"Maybe," said Melanie. She wrote it down.

After another fifteen minutes of this, Faye sighed and pushed the computer away. "This is not working. We have no idea what else they have in common. The themes aren't connected. We know they probably have different people in each group, unless we're looking for one random person who happens to be in both parades, and that's going to be tough to find."

Melanie and Kate nodded.

"Plus, all the things they have in common – every other parade has it, too. Route, bands, float signs, horseback riders, whatever. There doesn't seem to be anything that sets these two apart."

"Well, it was fun, folks," said Kate, lowering to the floor. She lay down with her feet propped up on the wall. Faye sat down beside her and began absently chewing a nail.

Melanie pulled the laptop toward her. "I'm not giving up yet." She clicked through pictures while Kate flexed her feet back and forth in the air.

Kate watched Faye continue to gnaw on her nail. "That's such a gross habit, Faye."

"Sorry." Faye pushed her hand by her side. "It helps me think."

"I think you're going to need more than nail-chewing to figure this one out."

"Guys," said Melanie, "take a look at these pictures."

Faye crawled over while Kate flipped onto her stomach. They both peered over Melanie's shoulder.

"What about them?" asked Kate.

"These are some floats from last night. And here," she clicked, "are some from the Aztecs. Do you see any similarities?"

"Um, no," Kate said.

"Compare it to one of the parades without weird letters." Melanie pulled up new pictures.

"You know," Faye said, "those floats do seem a little different."

"Yeah," said Kate, "they're kind of... boxy. Not as fancy."

"Exactly," said Melanie, switching back to pictures of the Aztecs and Centaurs parades. "In the parades with backwards letters, the floats are higher, and – oh, I don't know the right word."

"Poufy," supplied Faye.

"Yes!" said Melanie. "They're poufy. Curvy. They don't exactly look the same, of course, but they're similar."

"So what does that mean?" asked Kate finally.

"Maybe," said Melanie slowly, "we're dealing with the same float designer."

"Two parades…" said Kate.

"But one designer?" said Faye.

"Could be," said Melanie, her eyes shining. "So, the question is, who's our mystery designer?

MAGGIE M. LARCHE

# 3

That evening, Melanie sat down to dinner with her family. She, Faye, and Kate had spent the afternoon searching online for information on float designers, to no avail. Finally, they agreed to pump their families for information that evening.

"Mmm," said Melanie as her father set a plate of chicken and dumplings before her. "Smells good."

"Thanks, sweetie," said Mr. Smythurst. He had a kind face and messy brown hair.

"Here you go, Lacey." He set a My Little Pony plate littered with dumplings in front of the girl. "Use your fork, ok?"

Lacey nodded, and quickly hid the finger she'd dipped into the sauce. Melanie sighed. She knew it was only a matter of time before she found herself wearing Lacey's chicken and dumplings.

Everyone said the blessing and began to eat. Melanie considered the best way to approach the subject of the Mardi Gras parades while Lacey launched into a long explanation of a book she'd read at school.

"But the whole time, Princess Mia was hiding at the ball," Lacey finished with giggles. "That was really funny. I wish I was Mia." She turned to Melanie. "Call me Mia, ok?" she asked. "No!" She held up her hands. "Call me Princess."

"Whatever, Princess," said Melanie, while her dad winked at her over Lacey's head.

"So, Mel," said Mrs. Smythurst, "what did you girls do today?"

Melanie paused, planning her words carefully. "Well, we looked at some pictures of last night's parade."

"Oh, yes?" said her dad. "From what your mother told me, I'd have thought you got enough of that at the parade itself."

Melanie frowned. Maybe she shouldn't have been quite so open about her Mardi Gras fatigue last night. It would certainly make today's interrogation a little easier.

"No," Melanie finally said. "Well, sure, the parade was ok, I guess. It's just that this year, for the first time, I really noticed the floats themselves. Like, how they were made. They're actually really artistic."

Her mother nodded. "You're right, dear. It's hard to see them when they're moving so quickly in a parade, but they really are works of art." She smiled at Mr. Smythurst. "I remember how we used to love going to float inspection each year."

"Float inspection? What's that?" asked Melanie.

"Well, you won't remember this, Mel-Bel," said her father, "but back when I was in the Aztecs, every year they'd have a sort of family day, when everyone could come out to the float barn and see all the floats up close before the parade night."

"You were in Aztecs?" said Melanie in surprise.

"Sure," said her dad. "You knew that."

"Did not," said Melanie.

"Well, I guess you were pretty little at the time."

"Say, Dad, do you remember who designed your floats?" Melanie noticed her parents looking at her with perplexed faces. "I mean, I'm interested. They were really gorgeous last night."

"Sorry, hon, I don't remember," said Mr. Smythurst. "I wasn't heavily involved in the organization. We mainly showed up for parades and parties. Plus, it's been quite a while. Even if I remembered, chances are, it's someone else now."

He got up from the table to get seconds, and Melanie slumped in her chair.

"Shouldn't be too hard to find out, though," he continued, sitting down. Melanie sat up again. "There are really only a few people in town who do it."

"You mean, one float designer might work in more than one parade?" Melanie asked, trying to hide her excitement.

"Oh, sure," said Mr. Smythurst. "In fact, they're bound to."

"Lacey!" exclaimed Mrs. Smythurst, just as Melanie felt something wet slide down her arm. She looked down. Yep – a dumpling.

"Come on, sweet girl," said her mother, removing Lacey from the table. "Let's clean you up." She tossed a dishtowel to Melanie on her way out. "Sorry, hon. World's best big sister!"

"Yeah, yeah," said Melanie.

After dinner, Melanie texted Faye and Kate with news from the evening's dinner conversation.

*Dad says one designer will work on more than one parade. Doesn't know who though.*

Moments later, she received a response from Faye. *My parents either. Told me to look in the yellow pages. They're so old!*

After a few minutes, Kate joined in.

*Parents are out for the night. I'll hit them up tomorrow.*

*At least we've got somewhere to start,* texted Melanie. *Meet tomorrow @1. Faye's?*

*Faye's!* texted Kate.

*Yay!* sent Faye.

The next morning, Melanie filed into church with her family. She searched out Kate as she always did to wave hello. The two families had attended the same church for years.

Melanie spotted Kate sitting a few pews behind them. Kate and her brother Matt were thumb-wrestling while their parents were busy corralling the younger brothers. Melanie waved as unobtrusively as possible to get Kate's attention.

Matt had just defeated Kate and was wiggling in what Melanie assumed was his victory dance, albeit one constrained by being in a church pew. Kate crossed her arms and glared at him. Melanie waved her hand again to get their attention. Matt noticed her first. He grinned when he caught her eye and waved. Then he nudged Kate and nodded toward Melanie.

When Kate saw Melanie, all the disappointment at losing the game vanished from her face. She actually looked… excited?

She mouthed something quickly to Melanie.

"What?" Melanie mouthed back silently. Slowly, Kate repeated herself, and Melanie watched carefully to catch the meaning.

"I've. Got. A. Name."

Melanie's eyes widened. Could she mean the identity of the float designer?

Just then the opening song started up, and Melanie was forced to face the front. She fidgeted all through the service. If Kate really had the name of the float designer, they could get straight to work.

When the deacon finally announced that Mass was ended, Melanie said, "Thanks be to God," as fervently as she ever had and quickly led the way out of the pew. She threaded through the crowd and found Kate.

"Tell me everything!"

"All right," said Kate. "His name is Mr. Simmington, Josh Simmington, I think, and apparently he's ancient. He's been building floats for the Centaurs for a long time."

"Awesome! How did you find out?"

"He's one of my mom's clients," said Kate. "I think she did his will, though she couldn't come right out and say it. Attorney privilege and all. Still, small world, right?"

"Small town, anyway," said Melanie.

"Kate," said Matt, interrupting. "Mom said to come on." He grinned at Melanie. "Hi, Mel. You guys must have something exciting going on. Katie's been jumping up and down all morning."

"Have not," said Kate.

Melanie smiled at Matt. "Nothing exciting here."

"Yeah, I bet."

"I'd better run," said Kate. "I'll see you at Faye's!"

"What was your hurry?" asked her mother as Melanie rejoined her family.

"Nothing," said Melanie. "Just wanted to say hi to Kate." They walked to the parking lot.

"Want to stop for doughnuts on the way home?" asked Mr. Smythurst, unlocking the family van.

"Dad, I need to get home," said Melanie, before thinking better of it. Doughnuts were doughnuts, after all. "Well, ok, maybe a quick stop won't hurt."

"Yippee!" shouted Lacey from her car seat.

Half an hour later, Melanie licked sugar off her fingers as she walked down to Faye's.

On the way, Kate ran out of her house and joined Melanie on the sidewalk. "I texted Faye after Mass, so she's up to date."

"Good work," said Melanie. "I can't believe how quickly you found that name. You should be a detective."

"I don't know. It's kind of a lot of work." She massaged one of her hands as they approached Faye's porch. "Man, I think Matt sprained my thumb."

Melanie laughed and rang the doorbell.

Faye opened the door. "Hey, guys," she said, pulling the door shut behind her. "Let's go for a walk. Dad's got public radio blasting in the house." They turned down the sidewalk.

"So, Mr. Simmington," said Melanie, rubbing her hands together.

"Mr. Simmington," repeated Faye. "Well, I've done a little research."

"Of course, you have!" said Kate.

Faye continued on, pretending not to hear. "After I got the text this morning, I searched for him online. He's got a website, but it's basically just his name and a picture or two of floats. The site didn't list which parades he works on, but it did have a phone number. No email or anything."

"So maybe we should call him," said Kate.

"And say what?" asked Melanie. "We can't come right out and tell him we're trying to crack his code."

"If it is a code," said Kate.

"Of course it's a code," said Melanie.

"Maybe he wants someone to crack it," said Faye.

"If so, why did he make it so difficult?" asked

Melanie. "No, I think we'd better keep a low profile. We could tell him we're doing a report for school or something."

"Yeah," said Faye, "that's a good one. We could say we have to write a report about a local person who's contributed to the community."

"Just like those lame Citizen Reports we wrote last year," said Kate. "I wrote mine about the school lunch lady."

"Ms. Sue?" asked Faye.

"No, Ms. Leona."

"The mean one?" asked Faye in surprise.

"The mean one," confirmed Kate. "But ever since I selected her as my special Citizen, she's a big marshmallow to me. She always gives me extra helpings of chocolate pudding now."

"That's true," said Faye thoughtfully. "You do get more pudding than me."

Kate shrugged. "You just gotta play your cards right. And that's what we'll do with Mr. Simmington. Once he hears we've selected him for our report, he'll love us."

"He said, 'no thanks,'" said Kate, one minute later.

She'd gone inside her house to make the call to Mr. Simmington, while Melanie and Faye lounged on the back porch in the sun.

"What?" they both cried.

"I thought you were going to butter him up," said Melanie.

"I really don't know what happened." Kate sat down beside them. "He was nice and polite and all that. He said thanks for choosing him, but no thanks. And that was it."

She looked at Faye and Melanie.

Melanie felt as if someone had slammed a door right on her nose. "What did he sound like?" she asked.

"I don't know. What's an old float designer supposed to sound like?"

"I mean, did he sound busy?"

"Not really. Just not interested in being interviewed. Seriously though. Who doesn't like to be interviewed? Everyone loves to talk about themselves."

"Well," said Melanie. "I guess Mr. Simmington doesn't. If he won't talk to us, we'll have to get our information from somewhere else. But where?" She groaned and absently dragged a stick across the concrete floor of the porch. They'd had one breakthrough after another, but now she just felt stuck.

"We don't really know anybody in the organizations, right?" Melanie asked. Faye and Kate shook their heads. "My dad told me this morning that he used to be in Aztecs," she continued, "but it was years and years ago. He hasn't kept up with people in the group since then."

"Well, somebody knows about Mr. Simmington," said Kate in exasperation. "I mean, I know everyone keeps their Mardi Gras stuff hush

hush, but it's not *really* a secret, right?"

"I don't know about that," said Melanie slowly. "The whole focus is kind of on the mystery of it all. Think about it." She started counting on her fingers. "They wear masks during the parades. In all my searching for parade pictures, I had to rely on photos uploaded from the crowd. No group actually posted their own photos online. I didn't find any membership lists. I didn't even know my own dad was in a group until this morning."

She sighed. "What we need is someone who's made this kind of information their business."

"Wait a minute," said Faye. She sat up and held her hands out. "Wait, wait, wait…"

"What?" asked her friends.

"I've got an idea." Faye pumped a fist in the air. "Yes, that's it! The Mardi Gras museum! They're devoted to this stuff."

Melanie stared at Faye. "Faye Ryan, you are a genius. Why didn't we think of that before?"

"Well, let's go," shouted Kate, jumping to her feet. "It's not that far from here. We could probably make it on our bikes in twenty minutes."

"Just let me run tell my parents," said Faye.

"I'll go grab my bike," added Melanie. "Be back in a sec."

Melanie flew down the street to her house. They were moving forward again!

The three girls met up at Kate's house and took off down the sidewalk. Kate had plugged the address into her phone, and, as they rode, she shouted out directions to Melanie in the lead.

It was a beautiful day, with cool air and a brisk breeze, but Melanie could still feel the hot Mobile sun that was never far at bay beating down on her shoulders as she rode. By the time they pulled up in front of the museum thirty minutes later, she sighed in relief.

"Ok, I'm hot," she said, dropping off her bike and onto the front steps of the museum. Technically called the Mobile Carnival Museum, the museum had been established in an old historic home. Two porches lined the front of the building, one downstairs and one on the balcony, each with wrought iron facades. Two statues of masked revelers stood guard on either side of the front door.

Kate put her feet down beside her bike and pulled her hair into a messy bun atop her head. She fanned herself as she caught her breath. "Yeah, definitely sweaty. Yuck."

Faye pulled out a bike lock and secured the bikes to the wrought iron railing. "Think that's ok? There's no bike rack."

"Who's going to steal a bike on a Sunday?" asked Melanie. Suddenly, she stopped and smacked a hand to her forehead. "What am I thinking? It's Sunday!" She bounded up the steps to the door. "Please please please tell me you're open today!"

She tried pulling the door. "No!" she groaned, "It's locked!" She peered closely at the sign announcing the museum's hours. "Sunday: Closed," she read aloud. She turned to the girls who each stared at her with stricken expressions. Suddenly her legs felt ten times as tired. She sank to her bottom and leaned her back against the front door.

"Closed?" whispered Faye. "We rode all that way for nothing?"

"Oh, geez," said Kate. "I need shade." She climbed the steps and sat down beside Melanie against the door.

"I should have thought of this before we left," said Melanie. "I was just so excited. Why do we keep hitting all these dead ends?"

"Another closed door," grumbled Kate.

Just then, the door behind them opened, and Kate and Melanie fell backwards into the cool interior of the Carnival Museum.

# 4

Faye leaned over laughing helplessly while Kate and Melanie tried to untangle themselves from each other.

"I am so sorry!" they heard a voice from overhead.

Melanie looked up to find herself staring into the face of a young woman in trendy black frames.

"I didn't know anyone was sitting there," she said, reaching down to help them up. "Are you girls ok?"

Kate finally got her feet under her and reached her hand out to Melanie. She and the woman pulled Melanie up off the porch.

"No harm done," said Kate. "Melanie broke my fall."

Melanie glared at her and rubbed the back of her

head. "Yeah, we're fine," she added.

"Did you girls need something?" the woman asked. "You're welcome to sit on the porch, of course, but it's not the most exciting place." She lowered her voice. "Do you need to use the bathroom?"

"What?" asked Melanie. "No. That is… no thanks. We were looking for some information on Mardi Gras. Do you work here?"

"Yes. Well, sort of. I'm an intern," she said. "We're closed today, but I come in on Sundays and tidy up the exhibits. Plus I'm doing some of my own research, and the curator lets me poke around in my off time."

The three girls looked at each other and an unspoken thought flashed between them.

"You are just the person we wanted to see," said Kate. "Turns out I need to use the bathroom after all. Is it this way?" And she barged inside the museum, with Melanie and Faye scurrying meekly in her wake.

"Um, come on in," the woman said after them. She seemed a little confused.

"Thanks," said Faye, turning to the woman after they entered. "I'm Faye, and this is my friend Melanie. Kate's the one who's using the bathroom. Thanks for that, by the way."

"Nice to meet you. I'm Sasha Tipton."

"Wow," said Melanie, looking around. "This place is pretty cool. I've never been here before." She walked up to a display of a dress worn by a Mardi

Gras queen. The train stretched at least 15 feet, and sequins or jewels glittered along every inch.

"Please tell me those stones are not real," said Faye, walking next to Melanie.

Sasha laughed. "Only some of them. As you'd expect, that train is incredibly valuable. It cost the family $120,000."

"$120,000?" exclaimed Melanie. Even with her limited exposure to money, she knew $120,000 counted as a ton of money. That would buy her a lot of new books.

"Yes," said Sasha. "It's amazing what lengths people will go to in this town."

"Amazing," echoed Kate. Melanie hadn't noticed her walk up behind them. "Thanks for letting me use your bathroom."

"Sure," said Sasha. "You'd be hard pressed to find a public restroom open around here on a Sunday."

"Oh, what is that?" gushed Faye, pointing across the room to a large headdress. Sasha walked along with her to explain.

"Good move on the bathroom," whispered Melanie. "It got us in."

"What move?" asked Kate. "I really had to pee." But she grinned. Melanie laughed, and they walked over to Sasha and Faye.

"Were you about to leave?" Faye asked. "We don't mean to keep you, but..."

Melanie jumped in. "But if you have just a second, we'd really like to ask you a couple of questions."

Sasha raised her eyebrows. "Well, ok, I'll help if I can. It's always nice to meet people who are interested."

"We've been researching float design," began Melanie. Sasha's face registered surprise, but she kept silent. "And it turns out, we're big fans of Mr. Simmington's floats."

"Wow," said Sasha. "You have been doing research. You know Mr. Simmington, hmm?"

"Just know *of* him," said Melanie, quickly. "But we really like his floats that we've seen so far – the Aztecs and the Centaurs," she said with a stab in the dark. She felt heartened when Sasha didn't contradict her, but simply nodded along in confirmation. "And we were wondering," she continued hurriedly, "if you knew of any other parades he designs for, so we can make a point to go and see them."

"Sure," said Sasha, "I can help you with that."

"You can?" exclaimed Melanie. She could sense both Faye and Kate beside her tense up with excitement.

"Sure," said Sasha. "Mr. Simmington's practically a legend in Mardi Gras circles. He's been building floats for at least... oh, I'd say 40 years." She held up her hand and began rattling off her fingers. "Let's see, nowadays he does Ancient Aztecs, Centaurs, Apollo's Crewe, Mystic Shades, and Queen Hera's Court."

Melanie hurriedly typed the three new parades into her phone. "Apollo's Crewe, Shades, Queen

Hera." She looked up. "Wow, thanks a lot, Sasha," she said. "We didn't know how else to get the info."

"We tried to call Mr. Simmington and ask," said Kate, "but he didn't want to talk."

"I'm not surprised," said Sasha. "He's a very private man. Kind, but private. I get the impression that he prefers to let his floats do the talking for him." She leaned back against the table. "I'm glad to see you girls taking an interest. Seems like most kids just want moon pies and beads. What's got you on float design? It's an unusual subject for girls your age."

The girls exchanged glances.

Faye began, "Well, we were at the Centaurs parade, and we noticed –"

Melanie cut her off. "We just noticed how pretty the designs were, and how much work must have gone into them." She smiled and pointed at Kate. "Kate's an artist. She picks up on these things."

"I am?" said Kate. "I mean... I am." She nodded solemnly.

"Anyways, thanks for your time, Sasha," said Melanie, moving toward the door. "We'd never have gotten this far without your help."

"Glad to help," said Sasha.

Faye and Kate echoed Melanie's thanks, and all three girls trooped back onto the front porch.

Sasha followed and locked the door behind her. "You girls give me a call here at the museum if you have any more questions. And enjoy Mr. Simmington's floats. It's your last chance as I've heard he's retiring next year."

"We will," said Melanie. "Thanks."

The girls waved as Sasha descended the steps and turned down the street.

"Ok," said Faye to Melanie, putting her hands on her hips. "What was that about? Why did you stop me mentioning the code? She might have had some ideas for us."

"I don't know," said Melanie. "It just feels like it should be a secret." She started walking distractedly down the front steps. "It's like what we were talking about earlier. Mardi Gras is full of secrets. Why shouldn't we have one, too?"

"But we've already asked people for help," said Faye.

"Yeah," said Kate. "I got Mr. Simmington's name from my parents. And Sasha told us which parades he designs."

"Those are just clues," said Melanie. "Coming straight out and telling people about the code wouldn't feel the same. This is our puzzle. Just ours." She looked at her friends. "Can't we at least try? Just us?"

Kate smiled, and Faye nodded.

"Just us," agreed Faye.

"Our own Mardi Gras mystery," said Kate.

Melanie grabbed them both in a quick impulsive hug. "Exactly," she said. "And you know what?" She pulled back and smiled with suppressed excitement. "I think we just might solve it, too."

# 5

The next morning, Kate and Faye joined Melanie as she walked her little sister Lacey to preschool. Every school day, Melanie dropped Lacey off one block away before heading back to her own street to catch the bus.

Typically, Faye and Kate met Melanie when she returned from dropping off Lacey, but Melanie asked them to come along on the walk that morning. It was a good chance to talk without being overheard.

"We've got some issues," was all she would say. The girls dropped their backpacks off on the sidewalk and headed down the street.

Kate's twin brother Matt tried to follow them at first. Matt was as tall as Kate and had no problem catching up to the girls quickly.

"Katie," he called, jogging up behind them.

"I've told you a million times, do not call me Katie," said Kate. "And not now, Matt. We need to be alone."

Lacey peered at Matt from Melanie's side and grinned. "Hi, Matt."

"Hey, Lacey," he said, slowing to a stop. "How about I help walk you to school today, too? Kate wants my company, I can tell."

Melanie stifled a small laugh, and Matt looked pleased. Kate, however, was not amused.

She pulled Matt's arm and forced him to face her. "Seriously. Go back to the bus stop. We're busy."

"You're busy... what, walking?" Matt glanced around at the girls and whistled. "What's up, ladies? Everyone looks so serious. Don't tell me. Boy trouble." He sighed and shook his head. "Isn't that always the way?"

"Go back, or I'll tell Mom."

"Tell her what? I'm trying to be a good citizen here. Lacey wants me to walk with her."

"I'll tell Mom you let the dog take a bite out of her birthday cheesecake."

Matt's eyes widened. "No way. You wouldn't."

Kate nodded her head. "You bet I would."

"Katie, you promised."

"Don't call me Katie."

"Fine. But whatever you girls are cooking up, I bet you want my help before it's all over." He turned back to the bus stop.

"Don't count on it," said Kate.

The four girls started off again.

"Matt's not coming?" asked Lacey. "Why? I like Matt."

"You like everyone," said Melanie.

"I also like cheese," said Lacey. "And cake." She held Melanie's hand and skipped as they progressed down the sidewalk.

"And apples and peanut butter and spaghetti," she continued in a singsong voice.

"Ok, Mel," said Faye. "So what's the problem?"

"I checked the parade schedule last night," said Melanie. "One of the parades is on Friday – that's the Shades. Then, Apollo's Crewe is on Saturday, and Queen Hera is on Monday."

"The Big Finish," mused Kate.

"Yep," said Melanie. "But it's the Saturday parade that's going to be the problem."

"Of course!" said Faye, throwing a hand to her forehead. "The Kiwanis thing."

Melanie nodded.

Months earlier, the girls had formed a group for the school history fair. Due more to Faye's obsessive perfectionism than any contributions from Kate or Melanie, the girls had been one of the top projects selected to present at a local Kiwanis meeting.

"Is that this Saturday?" asked Kate.

"How could you forget?" asked Faye.

"Well, when *you're* doing all the work, it's easy for *me* to lose track."

"I didn't have to be the only one doing the work, you know."

"No way," said Kate. "Anytime I try, you just redo it. I've learned my lesson. This whole thing seems pointless, anyhow. Why do the Kiwanis people even care about a kids history project?"

"Because they're old," said Melanie. "Old people like history. Still, I don't know why they had to schedule it during Mardi Gras. Talk about bad timing."

"I know," said Faye, breaking in. "But we've got to do it. My mom was so proud when we were selected."

"What's selected mean?" asked Lacey.

"Picked, Lace." Melanie turned to her friends. "Getting back to the point of all this – we've got to go to the meeting, which means we miss the parade. And if we miss the parade..."

"We miss the letters," said Faye.

"Exactly."

"Melanie," said Lacey. "I'm super tired. Carry me. Please."

"Oh, all right," said Melanie with a sigh. She hauled her sister onto her back and trudged along.

"Can just one of us skip the meeting?" asked Kate. "You don't even need me. I won't know what to say to those people."

"What would be your excuse?" asked Melanie.

"I could pretend to be sick."

"And then your parents would let you go out to a parade instead? I doubt it."

"Yeah, I see your point. That's out."

They had arrived at Lacey's school.

"Be right back," said Melanie. She walked inside with Lacey. She came back out one minute later without her little sister, swinging her arms to work out the kinks.

"Man, Lacey's getting heavy."

The three girls turned back up the street.

"Seeing the upcoming parades is only one issue, though," said Melanie. "We've got another problem."

"What?" asked Kate.

"I bet I know," said Faye. "The Aztecs parade, right?"

Melanie nodded.

"What? I don't get it," said Kate.

"We've already missed it," said Melanie. "The Aztecs rolled last week. Now we need to find some way of getting the letters from the parade."

"But I thought you found pictures online," said Kate.

"Only of some of the floats. It's just random pics uploaded by people. There aren't pictures of every single float, every sign. And without seeing every one, how can we be sure we're catching all the letters?"

"And what about the beginning of the Centaurs parade?" added Faye. "We were at least halfway through before Mel spotted the first backward letter."

"I didn't even think about that," said Melanie. "Good catch, Faye."

Faye smiled modestly, but looked pleased.

"So," said Kate, ticking off on her fingers, "we've got one parade that's already rolled that we need to see. That's the Aztecs."

"Right," said Melanie.

"One more parade that we saw, but we might not have caught all the letters – The Centaurs."

Melanie nodded.

"And three more parades yet to happen that we need to see. One which we can't possibly attend, because we'll be at the Kiwanis meeting."

Melanie nodded. "That covers it."

"Three more parades," said Faye. She looked at Melanie. "You know, for someone who hates Mardi Gras, you're really getting your fill of it this year."

"Don't I know it," said Melanie. "You should have seen my parents' faces this morning when I told them I wanted to go to the Shades on Friday. I think they'd have been less surprised if I told them I'd taken up yodeling."

Her friends laughed.

"I haven't even mentioned Queen Hera to them yet," said Melanie. "They're going to think I've had a personality transplant."

"Well, I see any easy solution to all of our problems," said Kate.

"You do?" asked Melanie. "What?"

"Get a time machine."

"Wow," said Melanie. "I can't believe I didn't think of that. Good news, Faye, we've practically got this solved."

"Someone's sassy," said Kate.

"Well, you should take this seriously."

"I am, Mel." Kate put on a schoolmarmish

expression. "*Seriously* speaking, I think I've got an idea. Well, for one of our problems, anyway."

The girls were approaching the bus stop again.

"Although," Kate continued, "I'm not happy about it. It's going to involve a little groveling, and we might have to bribe him."

"Bribe who?"

Kate pointed to the bus stop. Up ahead, her brother Matt was sitting on the ground with a group of his buddies playing some sort of card game.

"Matt?" asked Faye.

Kate nodded. "If we can't go ourselves, we need someone to go to the parade for us and gather letters. I think he's our best bet."

"But isn't he going to want to know why?" asked Faye.

"We don't have to tell him the details," said Kate.

"He's going to be curious," said Melanie. "What if he tries to horn in on our mystery?"

"I've still got the cheesecake story, and I am not above blackmail. So, what do you guys say?"

Faye and Melanie exchanged glances.

"Ok," said Melanie.

"Excellent," said Kate. "I'll ask him on the bus."

The bus turned the corner five minutes later, and all the kids at the bus stop quickly shuffled into a line. Kate pushed and shoved to get the girls right behind Matt in line.

"Sit with me today," she said to the back of his head.

"What? After the way you acted this morning — forget it."

"I've got a business proposition for you."

Matt glanced over his shoulder. "Fine. But you'll have to make it quick. I'm a busy guy."

There weren't enough seats for all four of them to sit together, so Faye and Melanie had to split from the other two. They watched as Kate and Matt took a seat a few rows ahead of them.

"Think he'll do it?" asked Faye.

"I hope so."

"Think we can trust him?"

"I hope so."

Kate and Matt huddled in the seat together the entire ride. Their heads were bent down, and Melanie got the sense they were arguing. Every now and then, Matt glanced back over his shoulder at Melanie, but he quickly turned back to the front each time he met her eyes.

Finally, the bus arrived at school. Melanie and Faye caught up with Kate when they stepped off the bus. Matt had already split for his classroom.

Melanie was glad to see that Kate was smiling.

"Success?"

"Success. He drove a hard bargain, but he's going to go to the parade on Saturday and make a note of any weird letters. He should have them ready for us by the time we get home from the meeting."

"And did he want to know why?" asked Melanie.

"Of course," said Kate. "But I didn't tell him."

"So, what's the price?" asked Faye.

"It was his turn to do the laundry this week. I've got to do it for him."

"Well, that's not really too bad," said Faye.

"Laundry for eight people – for a whole week – isn't too bad?" asked Kate.

"I take it back."

"We'll help you," said Melanie. "Laundry at Kate's house, every afternoon this week."

Faye nodded in agreement.

"Thanks," said Kate. She grinned. "Well that's one problem solved, and the day's just starting."

"Not bad," said Melanie. "Now if only we knew how to go back and see the parades that have already happened."

"Try not to think about it," said Kate.

"So helpful," said Faye.

"I'm serious. That's what my mom always tells me to do when I've got a problem like this. You think about other things while your subconscious mulls over the problem until, BAM, you suddenly think of a solution."

"I don't know how good my subconscious is at problem-solving," said Melanie.

"So we're supposed to not think about it?" asked Faye, raising an eyebrow.

"That's right," said Kate. "And while we're not thinking about it, we'll be thinking about it."

"That's confusing," said Melanie.

"Don't worry," said Kate. "It works. How do you think I came up with the idea to blackmail Matt?"

# 6

The beginning of that week proved a challenge for Melanie. In spite of Kate's instructions not to think about the code, thinking about it seemed to be all Melanie *could* do. Repeatedly, she found herself worrying over how to find the missing Aztec letters. She spent all of social studies on Monday brainstorming methods to track them down. All she had to show for her work by the end of the period was a list with exactly one item on it: a big question mark.

When she wasn't worrying about the parade that had already passed, she was eagerly awaiting Friday's parade – the Mystic Shades. She kept going back and forth on the best spot to stand to get a good shot of the letters. She discussed strategy with Faye so many times that Faye eventually banned her from speaking.

Meanwhile, her teachers expected her to pay

attention in class like someone who didn't have the most exciting adventure of her life unfolding around her. With a previously spotless record, Melanie was called out three times in math class for not paying attention.

As the week dragged on, however, Melanie began to lose momentum. She still couldn't think of a solution to find the letters from the earlier parades, and every moment that passed felt like she was slipping farther and farther from her goal.

Surprisingly, the bright spot of the week was her daily laundry date at Kate's. Since the girls had taken over the chore from Matt, he sometimes stuck around to watch them fold the mountains of clothing that piled up from the family of eight. Sometimes he teased and tortured them, of course – Kate, especially – but other times he entertained the girls with funny stories as they worked. On the whole, it was an enjoyable exercise after school each day.

Still, Melanie found herself returning in her thoughts to the letters. The Mardi Gras code, as she now called it, continued to occupy more and more of her mind.

On Thursday night, Melanie washed dishes, while Lacey sat beside her at the kitchen table. Her sister flipped through a book about outer space and simultaneously maintained a constant flow of chatter. Melanie had no idea how Lacey could do both at the same time, but somehow she managed.

Once when Lacey paused to draw breath,

Melanie thought she heard the doorbell above the sound of the running faucet. She wiped a stray soap bubble from her nose.

Moments later, Kate ran into the kitchen, dragging Faye behind her. Faye held her laptop.

"Mel!" Kate exclaimed. "Pause the dishes. I've got something to show you." She turned quickly to Melanie's mother who stood behind her. "If it's ok with you, that is, Mrs. Smythurst."

Melanie's mom smiled. "You'd better go, Mel. This looks urgent."

Melanie quickly switched off the water and dried her hands on a dishtowel. She followed her friends out of the room and down the hall.

"Wait," yelled Lacey. "Me, too." She scurried down the hall behind Melanie, her little legs pumping.

"No, Lacey," yelled Melanie.

"Mel," called her mother. "I don't think she'll get in the way."

"Oh, all right," said Melanie. "Come on, hurry up."

She dashed into her room with Lacey behind her.

Lacey climbed onto the bed, jumped into the air, and landed on her bottom. "Whee!" she said as she bounced down on the mattress.

Melanie hurriedly closed her bedroom door before turning to the girls.

"What is it?" she asked. "Must be something big."

"It is," said Kate, grinning, and she pulled Faye's laptop out of Faye's arms. "Look what I found." She tapped on the keyboard.

"Where's your email, Faye?" she asked. "I sent the link to you."

Faye reached over and clicked the mouse. "Here."

"Perfect. Thanks. Now, take a look at this."

Melanie and Faye leaned in to see the screen. Melanie felt Lacey pushing through her legs, so she pulled her up and held her on her hip.

They could see a video on screen. A crowd flashed across the frame, and then...

"No way," said Faye.

"Is that?" asked Melanie.

"Yep," said Kate. "It's the Centaurs parade. Someone videotaped the whole thing. Like, every second."

The girls watched as the first float crossed the screen, and Melanie recognized its decorations. With the crisp picture, they could spot every detail of the design.

"Look!" shouted Faye. "That *I* is crooked!"

"We'll be able to see all of them," said Melanie. "That's awesome, Kate! Good find."

"Ooh," said Lacey. "Those are pretty. I want to see the parade."

"You're seeing it now," said Melanie. She put Lacey down and rifled through her desk. She grabbed a pen and piece of paper, while Lacey crawled onto the bed to watch.

"What are we waiting for?" asked Melanie. "Let's find those letters."

Thirty minutes later, the girls had completed the set of letters for the Centaurs.

Melanie compared the list to the original list on her phone.

"I'm so glad you found that, Kate. There were six letters we wouldn't have known about."

"Of course, it still doesn't make sense," said Faye.

"Nope," said Melanie. "But we're a step closer."

She carefully folded up the list of letters and placed it in the top of her jewelry box. Then she ceremoniously turned the key in the lock.

"Too bad that guy didn't tape the Aztecs parade, too," she said, sinking back to the floor.

"I know," said Kate. "We've still got to figure out that little problem." She tapped her head. "But just give it time. Like I said, the method works."

Melanie heard a small snore from behind her. She turned.

"Oh, geez."

Lacey had curled up on Melanie's pillow and fallen asleep as the girls excitedly pointed out every backwards or upside-down letter they could find. Now she snoozed comfortably.

"She'd better not drool on my pillow."

"Oh, hush," said Kate. "I'd kill for a sweet little sister instead of my menace brothers. Matt included."

"He's useful, though," said Melanie.

"And cute," said Faye. She glanced at Melanie.

"Have you ever noticed that, Mel?"

"Huh?" asked Melanie in confusion.

"Gross," said Kate.

"I said he's cute," repeated Faye to Melanie. "Don't you think so? And I think he's got a little crush on you."

Melanie didn't know how to respond, but she didn't have to. Kate distracted Faye by throwing herself down on the bed and pulling a pillow over her head. Her voice was muffled as she said, "I do not want to hear this."

Faye checked her watch. "I think I'd better get home anyway. When I told Mom and Dad that I wanted to do another parade on Friday, they *strongly* hinted that I'd better spend my other evenings getting in a little study time. Besides, I've got to prep for the Kiwanis meeting." She looked at Kate and Melanie. "I don't suppose either of you is getting ready for our presentation, are you?"

"I've got to do the dishes," said Melanie.

"I've got to... do something," said Kate.

"That's what I figured," said Faye. "Come on, Kate. Let's go." She pushed Kate out the door.

Melanie walked Kate and Faye out before returning to the kitchen sink. Dropping her hands back into the sudsy water, she smiled, reflecting that they were at least a tiny step closer than they had been one hour before.

# 7

On Friday night, the Mystic Shades took to the streets, and people jammed dozens of city blocks. Melanie bounced up and down on her feet, feeling a ball of burning excitement churning in her stomach.

In addition to being one of the more crowded parades of the year, it was also Melanie's first chance to test her theory that all of Mr. Simmington's parades would contain pieces of the code. While fairly certain that Mr. Simmington was the link between the parades, she still cheered when she saw her first backwards letter of the night. The sight confirmed they were on the right track.

Surrounded by screaming children and spectators waving for beads, the three girls made a funny sight at the parade. They ignored all throws and instead scanned each sign and float for mixed-up letters. Kate and Faye yelled out letters, while Melanie made notes on her phone.

One week earlier, Faye and Kate would have wrestled over a single strand of beads. Now a pile of them could fall on either of their heads, and the girls would only push them away impatiently. They were on a mission.

A young couple stood next to the girls dressed in evening clothes. The man wore a black tuxedo with tails and a white tie and vest, while the woman wore a long, shimmery blue evening gown. They were clearly going to attend a Mardi Gras ball that evening after the parade.

The woman caught notice of the strange letters, too. Melanie heard her remark on a upside-down *T* to her date. It didn't seem to capture the woman's interest for long, however, as she shortly missed a backwards *N* that paraded by a few floats later. Melanie smugly input the letter into her phone.

By the end of the evening, the girls were in possession of another stream of letters to work into their code. They returned from the parade to sleep at Kate's. With all of her brothers, Kate's house was the loudest and most crowded of their three homes. However, it also had the most readily available junk food, so the girls usually selected it for sleepovers.

The girls fortified themselves with pizza and Coke and then barricaded themselves in Kate's bedroom. Whenever one of Kate's younger brothers came to the door to annoy them, Kate smacked the door hard with a well practiced hand, and the boy in question scurried off.

Melanie and Faye settled on the floor with their dinners, while Kate occupied the desk chair.

"Mmm," said Melanie, taking a bite of her pizza and closing her eyes. "I was starved. All that bike riding."

"I know," said Kate, taking a long gulp of her drink. "I didn't realize code-breaking would be so strenuous."

"When this is all over," said Faye, "let's treat ourselves to something special. Maybe we can get one of our parents to drop us off for a movie."

"Or we could get manicures," said Kate.

"Yeah," said Faye with a dreamy sigh. "Something luxurious."

"And relaxing," added Kate.

"What's wrong with you guys?" asked Melanie, staring demandingly from one to the other. "You sound like you're actually looking forward to being done with the code."

Kate shrugged.

"Maybe, just a teensy, tiny bit," said Faye.

Melanie shook her head. "You're crazy. You're both crazy. This is the most fun I've had in ages."

"That's your problem, Mel," said Kate. She kicked her feet up onto her desk. "It takes too much to qualify as excitement to you. Ordinarily, I'd be happy enough with the fact that we've got a four-day weekend. You, on the other hand, need a mysterious puzzle sent from the Mardi Gras gods to keep you happy."

"I do not," said Melanie. "Besides, you know

you love it, too."

"You're right," said Kate with a smile. "I do. I'm just saying it in case it's what Faye's thinking. She never speaks up for herself." She glanced at Faye who had been silent throughout the exchange.

"Hey! That's not fair. I'm just as into this as you guys are."

"Good," Melanie said. "So, let's add in our clues from tonight and see where we are."

She reached into her overnight bag and pulled out the list of letters from previous parades. Carefully, she copied the letters from the Shades parade onto her sheet.

Faye watched over her shoulder as Melanie completed the list.

"So," said Faye, "we've got Apollo's Crewe still to go – which Matt will get for us tomorrow night – and Queen Hera's Court will be on Monday."

"And," added Kate, "we need to figure out what letters were in the Aztecs parade."

"Then," said Melanie, "we've got to actually *break* the code. I still don't see much sense in all these letters. Do you guys?"

Faye and Kate stared at the list in silence for a few moments before shaking their heads.

"What if..." Kate said slowly.

"What?" asked Melanie.

"Well, what if it's always just nonsense? What if it's not actually a code at all? Maybe it's just, like, Mr. Simmington's trademark to put in crazy letters or something?"

Faye nodded her head, as if this thought had occurred to her, too.

Melanie, however, looked absolutely stricken. "No," she said. "Just no. After all this work, all this mystery, it's got to be more than that."

Faye spoke gently. "We should be ready for it, just in case that's all it is."

Melanie shook her head. "No. My instincts tell me something's going on here."

Faye and Kate exchanged what looked like a worried glance, but Melanie chose to ignore it.

"Now," said Melanie, soldiering on, "I've been thinking about our little problem – how to get the Aztecs letters, and I think I've got an idea."

"Really?" squealed Kate. "What did I tell you? I knew my method would work."

"Oh no," said Faye with a groan, "not the whole 'don't think about it' solution again."

"You can't argue with results, Faye," said Kate.

"Actually," said Melanie, "sorry, Kate, but I did think about this one. It's all I've been thinking about all week long. I totally bombed today's math test because of it."

"Oh, no," said Faye. "That was an important test."

"Whatever," said Melanie, clearly valuing the code above her grade.

"So, what's your great idea?" asked Kate.

"Well, remember when I told you that my dad apparently used to be in Aztecs?"

Both girls nodded.

"When he told me, my mom said something at the time about how they used to enjoy going to float inspection. Apparently, each organization lets people come to see their floats before the parade. All the floats are parked in big float barns, which are basically just warehouses, and people can walk around and look at the floats up close."

"You think we should go to the Aztecs float inspection?" asked Faye. "But you said inspection is before the parade. The Aztecs have already gone."

"Right," said Melanie slowly. "We can't go to float inspection. It's too late for that. But I thought, maybe, that we could go to the Aztecs float barn and inspect the floats ourselves."

"Who's going to let us in?" asked Kate in confusion.

"They're not going to let us just wander around their warehouse," said Faye. "Besides, I thought you were against asking for help."

"I am," said Melanie. "That's why I thought we could…" She looked at Faye and Kate in consternation before saying quickly, "We could do it in secret."

Faye and Kate remained quiet for a moment. Finally, Faye spoke.

"Are you suggesting what I think you are?" asked Faye. "Do you think we should break in?"

"Not break in, exactly," said Melanie. "More like sneak in. I'm sure we could get in without having to bash in windows or anything."

Kate and Faye looked at her in silence.

"It's just an idea," said Melanie.

"Yeah, it's an idea," said Faye slowly. She looked at Melanie with an incredulous expression. "A crazy one!"

"Hey!"

"Well, it is!" Faye stood up and began pacing the room. "We're not burglars, Mel. I'm happy to chase all over town hunting for clues, but I think I draw the line at breaking into buildings that aren't ours."

"Ok, geez, never mind," said Melanie.

"Do you know what my parents would do to me if we got caught?" said Faye, not listening. "And I can't take jail! You can't go to college with a record!"

"Calm down, Faye," said Kate. "No one's going to force any of us to do anything. Melanie was just making a suggestion."

"A crazy one!"

"Yeah, you said that already," said Mel, bristling. "I just can't think of any other way to get at those floats. They're pretty much done for the season, and we've got to think of something, or we're going to run out of time."

"Sorry, Mel, but I'm not willing to go to jail just to solve the Mardi Gras code, however much you care about it."

Silence fell in the room.

"Fine," said Melanie finally.

"Fine," said Faye.

"Ok," said Kate at last. "I've got a great idea. Let's take a break from codes, puzzles, crime, whatever. No more talk about the mystery tonight, ok?"

"Whatever," said Faye.

"Fine by me," said Melanie. They wouldn't look at each other.

"We could play cards," suggested Kate.

"Fine."

"Fine."

Kate looked back and forth at them and seemed to decide it would be better to find an activity that didn't require talking. "Or we could watch a movie."

"Fine."

"Fine."

"And to think," Kate muttered, "I said Faye never spoke up for herself."

Melanie and Faye maintained a cold aloofness towards each other the rest of the night. Kate sat between them on the bed, holding the popcorn and trying to keep the peace. When the movie finished, Melanie crawled into her sleeping bag with only a short goodnight. Faye and Kate shared the bed.

Normally, the three girls would stay awake for hours, whispering and giggling into the night. Tonight, a library would have been louder.

Melanie lay awake in her sleeping bag for at least an hour, wrestling with doubts.

What had this mystery done to her? Had she gone too far?

# 8

The next morning, Melanie woke up to sunlight streaming into Kate's room. The light purple walls looked clean and bright in the morning sunlight, and the slight early morning chill in the bedroom made Melanie want to snuggle down into her sleeping bag.

The previous night had been filled with nightmares. Melanie dreamt she joined the police force. On her first day on the job, she had to arrest Faye for robbing a bank.

"You can't arrest me," shouted Faye as Melanie led her away to a waiting police car. "You did this to me. I turned to crime because of you."

Kate stood nearby, tap dancing on the sidewalk and laughing as Melanie stuffed Faye into the backseat. "Just don't think about it, Faye. All your problems will go away."

On the whole, Melanie was glad to be awake.

"Mel?"

Melanie rolled over to see Faye looking down at her from the bed. She still lay covered up by blankets, but she looked alert. She'd whispered, so Melanie guessed that Kate was probably still snoozing.

"Morning," whispered Melanie. "Listen, Faye," she began before she lost her nerve, "I'm sorry about last night. I'm going overboard solving the code. I never should have asked you and Kate to do something as dangerous as breaking into a warehouse."

Faye smiled at her. "Thanks. I'm sorry, too. I flew off the handle at you. I'm just getting all this pressure from my parents lately about school and that stupid violin – did I tell you my mom wants me to join the debate team now? – and I guess the thought of getting caught by the police doing something illegal… well, it just sent me over the edge."

"That's fair," said Melanie. "And you're right. It is an insane idea. I really don't know what I was thinking."

"You were thinking that we have to solve this code. And you're right. We do."

Melanie sighed. "I have no idea how we're going to now. Besides, I wouldn't even know how to break into somewhere." She giggled quietly. "What would we do, run down to the hardware store and buy crowbars and masks?"

Faye laughed. "I'd have a hard time explaining that one to my mom."

Melanie smiled and rolled over. She stared up at the ceiling.

"You know, when we started all this, I didn't even really know what I was looking for." She sighed. "Life just seems so boring sometimes."

"I know. Everyone feels that way. At least, at times."

"But then, you find something like this, and you think, maybe it's not so boring after all." She rolled back to face Faye. "We're so close to solving this mystery. I hate that we might never know what it's all about. If we don't figure it out – that would just stink."

The girls lay quietly thinking. Finally, Faye spoke.

"You know," she said, "it probably wouldn't hurt anything just to go and look around."

Melanie wrinkled her forehead. "Go where?"

"The float barns, of course."

Melanie sat up, her sleeping bag pooling around her pajamas.

"Are you serious?"

Faye nodded. "I am not bringing a crowbar, of course, but maybe we could go nose around and see what we find. Without getting arrested."

Melanie felt a surge of excitement.

"I think it's time to wake up Kate."

Later that morning, the girls took off on their bikes. An especially cold day, Melanie's knuckles were stiff and chapped by the end of the long ride.

The three girls stopped their bikes at the corner

of a quiet intersection. Melanie tried to rub feeling back into her hands.

"Anybody else feel like they're about to be mugged?" asked Kate.

Melanie had to agree that the street did not form the most welcoming image. Large metal warehouses lined the road, some of them rusting around the edges. Nearby sprawled large empty fields, covered with dead grass waiting for spring to cover the rutted ground. Signs advertising bail bondsmen were the only decoration on the street.

"Let's get moving then," said Faye. "Which one belongs to the Aztecs?"

Melanie scanned the road. "I think it's that one," she said, pointing to a nondescript warehouse in the line. "If the pictures online were recent, it's the third one from this end."

"They all look the same," said Kate.

"We'll just have to hope our research is good," said Faye. She turned to the other two girls, leaning over one side of her bike. "Plan of attack. We need to circle the warehouse and get the lay of the land. Once we know what we're up against, we'll be able to figure out a way to get inside. Preferably one that is not illegal."

"I can't believe we're doing this," said Kate. She knocked her kickstand backwards and shook her head. "I can't believe *Faye's* leading the way."

The girls approached the warehouse slowly. From the street, Melanie thought it looked impenetrable. The building's large steel doors sealed the entrance, and the rest of the front was nothing more than a wide expanse of metal sheeting.

"Let's try down the side," said Faye, signaling for the girls to follow her.

They rode around the side of the warehouse, again seeing no possible way in. But at the back, they found more than they ever expected.

The three girls stopped their bikes and uttered a collective gasp.

"It's open!" said Faye.

The back of the warehouse had large steel doors mirroring the front. Unlike the front doors, however, these weren't completely closed. They stood about ten inches apart, a large rusty chain keeping the two doors from opening further.

They glimpsed black darkness just beyond the doors.

Finally, Melanie spoke. "This is great," she said. "We don't actually need to break in." She jumped off her bike and ran to the crack. "I think we can fit." She stuck her head inside. "And I see floats." She turned back to Faye and Kate. "Well? Do we go in?"

"Should we wait until nighttime?" asked Kate. The girls paused.

"I don't want to come back to this street in the dark," Faye finally said, voicing what all three girls were thinking. Melanie nodded.

Kate blew out a breath of air. "Then, I guess now it is. Should we lock our bikes?"

They looked around the deserted street.

"I don't see where we could lock them," said

Melanie.

"Besides," added Faye, "we might want them free to make a fast getaway."

Kate shook her head and groaned. "I am in an alternate universe."

Melanie grinned. "Come on, Kate. I can hear clues calling to me." She squeezed inside first.

Melanie blinked her eyes blindly. "It is really dark in here," she said aloud.

"I wish we could open the doors some more," came Faye's voice.

Kate's face lit up in the dark. "Have we forgotten something, ladies?" She held her phone's flashlight under her face and made a spooky expression.

"Duh," said Melanie, while she and Faye each pulled out their own phones. "Excuse me. I'm new to the world of crime."

She turned her phone flashlight to the nearest float and was met with the ten-foot-tall head of an ancient Indian warrior. She jumped.

"Good news," she said with a shaky laugh. "We've definitely found the Aztecs float barn."

Finding the letters turned out to be harder. Because of the darkness, the girls were forced to walk very slowly. Even with their phones, they had to strain to pick out details in the floats. Then, because they were focused on looking up at the floats, they kept missing things at their feet and stumbling. Kate, with her height, had particular trouble with this. Twice she tripped over extension cords running along the floor.

"Lift your feet," said Faye. "Like this." She pantomimed lifting her knees high in the air like a soldier.

"I am not walking like that," said Kate. "I'd rather trip."

They walked through the warehouse, examining each float and sign one by one, searching for any backwards or upside-down letters. Whenever they found one, they made a note of it in Melanie's phone, along with the corresponding float number to keep them in order.

The warehouse felt like a meat locker, and every now and then, Melanie thought she felt a small cold breeze down the back of her neck. She briefly entertained the thought that if someone were standing behind her in the dark, she'd never even know, before quickly shoving the thought out of her mind. The situation was spooky enough without her imagination making it worse.

They snaked up and down the rows, walking first towards the front of the warehouse before heading back down a row towards the back. They progressed up the final row and reached the last float.

Melanie examined the large float bearing a model of a medieval castle, when Kate suddenly popped up into view. She had climbed aboard the float.

"Kate!" said Melanie. "What are you doing?"

"Oh, come on," said Kate, grinning. "You're the one who told that Sasha girl that I'm an artist. Of course I've got to examine the float up close. It's part of my artistic temperament. Besides," she began a queenly wave to imaginary crowds below, "you can't say you've never wanted to climb on one of these."

"I have not," said Melanie.

"Well, I have," said Kate.

"Me, too," said a small voice, and Melanie swung her phone around to light up Faye.

"Faye! Not you, too."

Faye leaned out over the side of the float and examined the silver leaf detail along the edges of the fake stones. "I'm not going to get a chance like this again, am I?"

"This is so cool," said Kate. "I'm absolutely going to join an organization when I'm older." She disappeared below the side of the float. "Hey," her voice floated up, "there are no bathrooms on here. What do they do when they've gotta go?"

The girls started giggling, when they suddenly were cut short. The warehouse echoed with a loud clang, and the room filled with light.

Someone had opened the front doors.

# 9

Faye immediately ducked down, and seconds later, she and Kate rejoined Melanie at the bottom of the float. All three girls huddled behind the side of the structure, grasping each other's hands with frozen fingers.

Melanie felt waves of fear sweep through her. She stared at a paper mâché crocodile swimming in the float's castle moat, and felt as trapped as if she were in that moat herself.

They heard voices.

"Dang, it's cold today," said a deep voice with a thick southern accent.

"Yep," said another slightly higher male voice. "I'm glad we're not parading tonight. I was thinking about running the boat later, just to keep it up, but I'm sure as heck not going out in this weather."

The other man grunted in reply. "So," he said,

"which floats are they coming to get?"

"Please don't say the castle float," thought Melanie. "Don't, don't, don't."

"Uh… Knights of the Round Table," said the higher voice.

Melanie, Faye, and Kate looked at each other with wide eyes. Faye pointed to the castle float they were hiding behind, her eyebrows raised in question, and Melanie and Kate mutely nodded. Faye moaned softly.

"What now?" thought Melanie, biting her lip in anxiety. She felt a tug on her sleeve. Kate waved for her friends to follow her as she began walking in a crouch down the length of the float. Melanie and Faye quickly followed.

"How long 'til they get here?" asked the first voice.

"Can't be more than five minutes," said the second. "Let's go ahead and clear it out."

The girls began waddling faster down the row of floats. They had passed beyond the castle float, but the men would only have to look down the back row to see the girls plainly.

"Go, go, go," thought Melanie. They scurried along, panic rising in them.

They reached the end of the row and turned the corner. They hid behind the very last float. Melanie spotted one more backwards letter she'd missed before and made a mental note.

They could see the cracked back door. But to get to it, they'd be exposed for a few seconds. Where were the men?

Waiting was intolerable. Melanie felt like sticks were poking her insides as adrenaline coursed through her. She expected at any moment for one of the men to put his head around the corner of the float and demand to know what they were doing there. They had to make a run for it.

Melanie motioned for Kate to go first.

Kate took a deep breath and took off for the opening. She slipped through the crack so silently that Melanie smiled.

She could hear the men talking again, and though they sounded closer than before, she was relatively sure that they were still near the front of the warehouse.

She motioned for Faye to go next.

Faye sprinted to the door. She slipped through quickly enough as well, but the chains rattled slightly on her way out.

"Did you hear something?" asked the man with the higher voice. "That was weird."

"What?"

"Sounded like it was at the back. I hope we haven't got another raccoon in here."

"Better check it out."

"They're coming," thought Melanie in a panic. She could no longer wait and took off for the door, feeling as if she were trying to outrun her own fear. She dashed through the opening, scraping her shoulder on the side of the door. She found Faye and Kate already seated on their bikes waiting for her.

Kate was holding Melanie's bike for her so Melanie only had to jump aboard. They all began pedaling madly. As soon as they reached the end of the next warehouse, they turned left so as to be hidden from the float barn's back door.

"OhmyGod, OhmyGod, OhmyGod," chanted Kate to the rhythm of her pedaling as they biked away at breakneck pace.

Two blocks later, the girls reached a city park. They cruised to a stop before crumbling onto the grass next to their bikes.

They panted heavily. Faye groaned weakly.

"*That's* why I didn't take to a life of crime. Pure fear."

"That was terrifying," said Melanie.

Another "Oh, my God," was all Kate could manage.

The girls lay on the ground, catching their breaths.

No one knew who started it, but suddenly all three of them were laughing. Great, deep belly laughs that communicated how great it was to be alive, and young, and not arrested for trespassing in the Aztecs float barn.

"I can't believe it," Kate finally said as their laughter died down. "We really did it."

Faye still giggled weakly.

"I know," said Melanie, staring up into the Spanish moss dangling from an enormous oak limb. "We did it, and we got just the clues we need." She held her phone up into the air. "Right here."

She rolled onto her stomach and looked at Faye and Kate. "What did I tell you? We're going to solve it. Nothing can stop us now."

Melanie arrived home that afternoon, tired but elated. She sailed upstairs to her room and pulled the door shut behind her. She unfolded the piece of paper with all the known letters and carefully added in the new ones.

She smiled down at her almost completed list. Tonight, she'd get the next batch of letters, and then there were only two more days until the final piece of the puzzle. She hoped.

The doorknob to her room turned. The door swung open a few inches to reveal Lacey, staring through the crack.

"Melly," whispered Lacey. "Can I come in? I'm hiding."

Melanie pulled the door open for her. In her current state of mind, she could even handle a little babysitting time.

"Come on, Lace," she said. She carefully locked her paper back into the jewelry box before taking her sister's hand.

"Are you going to play with me? Yay! Wanna paint?"

"I'll *color* with you," said Melanie, leading Lacey down the hall. "Last time we painted, you turned my nose red."

"Ok." said Lacey. "Color. With Mel." She skipped along Melanie's side.

That evening, Melanie and Faye met at Kate's house to ride to the Kiwanis meeting together. While they were waiting on the front porch for Kate's mother to drive them, Matt sauntered out.

"I see you guys are off to be studious while I do the dirty work. Typical."

Melanie looked at him seriously. "Are you ready for tonight, Matt? You've got to be sure to get every single letter. We need them all."

He grinned. "I've got it. I promise, nothing's gonna slip by me." He leaned against the wall. "So, one last chance. Does anyone want to give me a hint of what this is all about?"

"Nope," said Kate. "Just hold up your end of the bargain because I am about sick of laundry."

"Don't worry. I'll bring home the goods. The merchandise. The loot. The – "

Kate stopped him. "We get it, Matt."

"Don't forget," added Melanie, "if you stand right underneath the clock tower, you can get the best view of the floats."

"Melanie, I've been to a parade before."

"I know, I know. Sorry." She smiled at Matt. "Thanks for doing this for us."

Mrs. Butler came out of the front door. "Let's go, girls. Into the van." She stopped to plant a kiss on Matt's head.

"Mom!"

"Be safe at the parade. See you when I get home."

"Bye, girls," said Matt, waving cheerily. "Don't do anything I wouldn't do."

Melanie smiled as she watched him through the van window. Even though she didn't want to share the code beyond Kate and Faye, it was nice to have Matt as a partial member of the team. And Faye was right… he was a little cute.

"Ok, let's review for the presentation." Faye startled Melanie out of her reverie.

Melanie jumped and, for some reason, found herself blushing. "Sure. Fire away."

The Kiwanis meeting that evening was about what Melanie expected. Middle-aged men and women milled about the room, politely stopping to ask the girls questions about their projects. Faye answered them with ease, and Melanie and Kate nodded along as if they would have said the same thing if given the chance. Their history teacher cycled through the room and beamed at all the students.

Melanie was eager to be done with the evening and get her next set of letters. This mock presentation was a poor substitute for working on the Mardi Gras code, and she itched to leave. Her thoughts were firmly fixed on Matt. She kept glancing at the clock, estimating where the parade would be and how many letters Matt might have found by then.

When it was finally over, Melanie heaved a sigh of relief and helped pack up their presentation. They rode back with Kate's mother and dashed inside the house as soon as the van was parked.

"Where's Matt?" Kate asked her father as soon as they crossed the threshold.

"Not back yet," he said. He glanced at his watch. "I'm a little surprised, actually. But I'm sure he'll be home soon."

"Honey," Mrs. Butler called from the garage. Something in her voice caused everyone to look alert. "Come out here."

Mr. Butler hurried from the room.

"Look!" Faye shouted, running to the front window. Melanie and Kate were close on her heels.

A police car had pulled up in front of the Butler's home.

# 10

"Oh, no." Faye turned to her friends with a stricken face. "They're here for us. They know about the float barn. Oh, my God, what are we going to do?"

"How could they know?" cried Kate. "No one saw us."

"Let's go out the back door," said Faye. "Hurry."

"Faye," said Melanie. She rushed to stop Faye from leaving the room. "Calm down. We are not going on the run from the police. That's crazy."

"It's better than being locked up!"

"Wait," interrupted Kate. "Look. They're not here for us. They've got Matt!"

Melanie dashed back to the window. Sure enough, she could make out Matt through the darkness. He was climbing out of the backseat of the car, a somber looking policeman by his side.

"What happened?" she asked. "Is he ok?"

"You mean they're not here for us?" Faye put a hand to her head and weakly sighed. "Thank goodness."

"Thank goodness?" cried Melanie. "Matt's been arrested, and that's all you can say?"

"Sorry," said Faye. "I mean, poor Matt. I wonder what happened."

"We'll find out soon enough," said Kate, her nose still pressed against the window. The policeman handed Matt over to his parents, and the adults conferred together.

"They're coming in," said Kate. She retreated from the window and faced the door.

Moments later, Kate's parents and Matt walked into the room.

"Girls," said Mr. Butler, "run on up to Kate's bedroom, please. We need to talk down here."

Kate nodded, and the three girls shuffled out of the room. Melanie snuck a glance back at Matt on her way out. He was staring right at her, and he winked as soon as she met his eye. She felt the knot in her stomach loosen slightly, and she gave him a small smile before he vanished from view.

Upstairs in Kate's room, the three girls sat in stricken silence for a moment.

Finally, Kate broke the quiet. "I wish I could hear what's going on down there."

"Do you think he's really in trouble?" asked Melanie.

Kate raised her eyebrows and blew out a breath.

"It looks that way."

"What on earth could he have done?" asked Faye.

They stared at each other. No one had a good answer.

"Can you imagine if we'd been caught sneaking into the float barn this morning?" asked Kate. She put her hands on her forehead. "Geez, was that only this morning? What a day."

"Your parents would have had two cop visits in one day," said Faye, shaking her head.

"They would have died. After they killed me, of course."

The girls broke out into nervous giggles that quickly built into uncontrollable laughter.

"At least Matt didn't seem too worried," said Melanie, wiping her eyes as she calmed down, "so hopefully it's not too bad."

"Speaking of Matt," said Faye, "you certainly seemed concerned about him."

"What are you talking about?"

"What were your words?" She screwed up her forehead in thought.

"I remember," said Kate. "'Matt's been arrested, and all you can say is thank goodness?' Sounds like you care."

"Of course, I care," said Melanie with a hot face. "If he got arrested doing a favor for us, we all should care."

"It wasn't a favor," said Kate. "We paid him. Have you already forgotten all that laundry duty?"

"You know what I mean."

"Yes, I do," said Kate. "You mean you like him."

"Do not."

"Yes, you do," said Kate. "Ugh. One of my best friends likes my brother. What am I going to do?" She spoke in a light tone, but Melanie sensed an undercurrent of real concern behind her words.

"I do not," Melanie repeated.

"Leave her alone," said Faye.

Melanie was about to thank her, but there was a teasing look in Faye's eye that rubbed Melanie the wrong way. She crossed her arms instead and settled back on the bed.

Suddenly all three girls jumped from a knock on the door.

"Let me in." Matt's urgent whisper drifted through the door. Kate ran to open it. He hurried inside and pulled the door shut behind him.

"What happened?" said Kate. She hit Matt on the arm. "I can't believe you were arrested."

"Shh. Keep it down. Mom and Dad don't know I'm in here. I'm supposed to be in my room." He surveyed the girls and grinned. "I've got something for you." He pulled a piece of paper out of his pocket with a flourish. "Backwards, upside-down, and all around weird letters, for your reading pleasure. I have no idea what you're going to do with them, but then, I don't really get girls."

Melanie grabbed the sheet of paper with a cry. "Thank you, Matt. We owe you one."

"Do not," said Kate. "Laundry, remember?"

Melanie waved her off while she examined the list. She couldn't wait to add them to her master set.

"Ok, so tell us what happened," said Kate.

"I've gotta be quick," said Matt, but he settled onto the floor anyway. "I was doing fine, spotting letters – you guys have weird hobbies, by the way – but somewhere in the second half of the parade, this old lady scoots right next to me. Not a nice little old lady either."

The girls nodded. They knew even the sweetest elderly folks could turn vicious when fighting over Mardi Gras beads. It was a strange but well known fact.

"She was a tough one, and she was reaching and scurrying along with everyone else to grab stuff. I was minding my own business, searching for letters like a good private eye should, when on the very last float, this old lady jumps straight into me. We both fall over. She starts yelling about her hip or something, and then lots of people are there helping her up and stepping all over me.

"By the time I got up, the last float had already gone by. So, I tried to follow it down the side, but you know what Saturday parades are like."

"Packed," supplied Faye.

"Exactly. I couldn't move anywhere, but I knew I needed to check that float. So, I did the only thing I could. I jumped the barricade."

"You what?" exclaimed all three girls.

The first rule of Mardi Gras that every Mobile child learned was to never cross the barricade. If you jumped over the metal partitions separating the crowd from the floats, it would mean only one thing – you were going to be arrested.

"I had no choice. You said you needed every single letter, so I had to make sure. So there I was, running down the street after the float, dodging horse poop, by the way, which was gross. I'd just caught up to the last float when the cop nabbed me. But it was a good thing I ran after it, because I spotted one more letter right when the guy started dragging me off."

The girls met his story with awed silence. Melanie stared at him with wide eyes. She couldn't believe that he had gone to such lengths for them.

"What happened to the old lady?" asked Faye finally.

Matt grunted. "I saw her walking away from the parade with a bag full of stuff. Her hip or whatever was just fine."

"Matt," said Melanie, "thanks. Really. We feel awful that you got in trouble for this."

Matt smiled. "No big deal. I had to help you."

Melanie suddenly felt shy. She wasn't able to meet his eye, and she saw Faye and Kate glancing back and forth between the two of them.

"I better get home," she said, standing up. "After all that, I don't want to lose these." She waved the piece of paper in the air, looking at her feet.

"See everyone tomorrow." She quickly left the room, and ran down the stairs and out the front door.

# 11

Sunday, or Joe Cain Day, was a special day in Mobile. On this local holiday, Mobile celebrated the reemergence of Mardi Gras after the Civil War. The day and its parade had been named after Joe Cain, the man who was credited with bringing back Mardi Gras to the battle-weary town.

Now, Joe Cain Day was possibly the most popular day of Mardi Gras, rivaling even Fat Tuesday itself. Much of the city turned out for the day's parade, which was unique among the season's many festivities. While most Mardi Gras parades were run by mystic organizations with professional floats, Joe Cain was the people's parade. It included marchers, homemade floats on the flatbeds of trucks, and ordinary citizens of Mobile throwing to the crowds.

Many of the families on Melanie's street spent

Joe Cain day together every year. They'd head out early to the parade route and claim a large section for the neighborhood to watch together.

People brought chairs and music and drinks. Families contributed steaming pots of gumbo and large Igloo coolers full of red beans and rice to keep everyone fed. It was like a neighborhood block party, with the added fun of the Joe Cain parade as entertainment.

After church, Melanie and her family drove downtown. Her dad maneuvered the family minivan into a street parking spot, and they unloaded their gear. They began the walk to the parade route. Melanie juggled four fold-up chairs, while Lacey skipped along beside her.

It was a gray day. Though the population was predisposed to celebrate, the weather was not. Thick gray clouds blanketed the sky, and a warm, humid wind swept the city steadily. Melanie shook her head at the rapidly changing weather that always characterized winter in her town.

Melanie spotted Faye's family as they neared the barricades.

"Hey!" shouted Melanie, waving. Faye saw Melanie and came running up.

"Hi, Mr. and Mrs. Smythurst," she said, taking two of the chairs from Melanie. "Here, I'll help."

"Thanks, Faye," said Melanie's mother. "Your family arrived early."

Faye nodded. "You know Dad. He's like a kid at Joe Cain. He can't wait to get down here."

Mr. Smythurst rubbed his hands together. "I know just how he feels! Come along, ladies, I see a good spot."

Melanie and Faye fell back slightly as her parents and Lacey headed for the free space.

"Is Kate here yet?" asked Melanie.

"No, but she just texted that they're on their way."

Melanie checked her watch. She groaned. "I hate to waste a whole day. We're out here killing time when I just want to be working on the code."

"This isn't killing time," said Faye. "It's having fun. Take it from me. I know I can overdo the studying, but sometimes you've just got to take a day off. It'll be good for you. Besides, there's nothing we can do today anyways. We have to wait for tomorrow's parade to get the final clues."

"I know that, but some part of me just doesn't care. I can't stop thinking about it."

"Then we'll distract you," said Faye.

"How?"

"Easy. We are going to eat lots of gumbo. And drink about fifty sodas. Each. And dance to that ridiculous music my parents like to play on the radio." She looked at Melanie. "Maybe even spend some time with Matt," she added, "assuming his parents let him out of the house."

"Oh geez, my stomach already hurts."

"From the fifty sodas or Matt?"

"Mel," called Lacey. "Here's our spot." She waved Melanie over.

The day passed very quickly. Kate arrived shortly, and the three girls enjoyed themselves thoroughly. Good will permeated everything on Joe Cain Day. Even Kate's little brothers benefited from the rosy glow. The girls were inclined to find their antics throughout the day funny, rather than annoying.

In punishment for his run-in with the law, Matt had to stick close to his parents for much of the day. He did manage to slip away long enough to challenge Melanie to a round of beanbags.

Melanie was on pins and needles the entire time they played. She wasn't sure how to behave with Matt, and she caught Kate watching them more than once with a concerned expression. Matt seemed to be behaving normally, however, and after Melanie won, he congratulated her in his typical easygoing fashion before his parents called him back to their side.

Melanie breathed a sigh of relief, but just as quickly felt a small stab of disappointment. Nothing was simple anymore.

Later that afternoon, the parade began to roll. Melanie and her friends crowded the barricade along with everyone else. Lacey sneaked under people's legs to find a good spot by her sister. Melanie's parents stood just behind the girls.

Float after float drove by, interspersed with marchers and truck bands. Music blared, and everyone danced along, paraders and spectators alike. Some floats were obviously homemade, no more than trucks and trailers dressed up for the occasion.

A few groups had rented their floats from the established Mardi Gras organizations. Melanie jumped when she saw the Aztecs' "Knights of the Round Table" float that she and her friends hid behind. The three girls met eyes and giggled.

One particularly raucous float rolled through, and the riders dumped throws on the girls.

Faye reached out to catch a teddy bear when a large bundle of heavy beads caught her in the cheekbone.

"Ow!" she yelled, holding her hand to her cheek.

"Faye! Are you ok?" asked Melanie.

"No. I think I broke my face. Is that possible?"

"Better get ice on that, dear," said Melanie's mother. "I'll go grab some for you."

"That's ok," said Faye. "I'll get it. When you get walloped upside the head, I think it's a sign to quit."

She threaded her way back through the crowd toward her parents. Melanie saw Mr. Ryan put his arm around Faye while her mother ran for ice.

"Poor Faye," said Kate. "That looked like it hurt."

"For real," said Melanie. She turned back to the parade and spotted a black bus coming down the street, loaded down with her favorite characters of the day.

"Ooh," Melanie heard Lacey say. "Who are they, Daddy?"

"Those, little Lace, are Cain's Merry Widows."

The Merry Widows were a staple of the Joe Cain parade. Riding down the street in their long black dresses and dark veils, no one knew their true identities. They looked out from their black bus, throwing black beads, black roses, and black garters to the crowd.

She didn't exactly know why, but the Merry Widows were one part of Mardi Gras that always appealed to Melanie. When so many of the Mardi Gras revelers felt garish and silly, the Merry Widows seemed to Melanie to hit the right note of mystery.

"The Merry Widows pretend that they were married to Joe Cain," her father explained to Lacey. "They start every Joe Cain day out at his grave and wail and cry over it."

"Oh, no. They're sad."

"Not really, Lace. They're just pretending."

"I like to pretend," said Lacey. "Can I be a Merry Window?"

Melanie and her father laughed.

"Widow, not window," he corrected.

One of the Merry Widows leaned out of her bus window right then and tossed Melanie a set of black beads.

Melanie waved in thanks, while the widow disappeared mysteriously down the parade route.

The parade ended soon after the Merry Widows. A few more floats, some mounted policemen, and then the street cleaners barreled down the avenue. Melanie stepped back from the barricades as the crowd slowly began to disburse.

All around her, people compared what they had caught. Children grinned from the excitement or lay passed out on their parents. Melanie's mother stood and chatted with a group of women from their street. Her dad hopped along the road, making Lacey giggle as she bobbled from side to side on his shoulders.

Melanie felt a warm glow of wellbeing that had been missing from her life the past several weeks. She felt no thrill of mystery right now, just the happy contentment from a day spent in the company of her family and neighbors, celebrating life in a way that was unique to her city. Melanie hadn't even realized she'd been missing that feeling until its return.

"Great parade," said Kate, linking her arm through Melanie's. "And I can say that, even with the gazillions of other parades we've seen this year. So it must be true."

"It's hard to believe there's only one left to go," said Melanie. "I feel like we've been chasing down this mystery for months. But it's only been a week. And now we're down to the last one." Her voice held a curious mix of excitement and regret.

"Come on," said Kate. She nudged Melanie. "No getting sad."

"I'm not," said Melanie. "Not really." She looked ahead to their families. "You're right. It was a good day."

"That's the spirit."

"Let's go see how Faye's doing."

They found Faye talking with two of Kate's younger brothers. She held a Ziploc full of ice to her cheek, water dripping down her arm and onto the street. When she saw her friends, she came to meet them.

"Yikes," said Kate. "How're you feeling?"

"Not bad, surprisingly," said Faye. "The ice has numbed everything. But it's not going to look great over the next couple of days. Hey, listen." She motioned them to come closer. "Guess who I ran into while I was sitting here?"

"Who?" asked Melanie.

"Sasha Tipton!"

"From the Mardi Gras museum?"

"Yep. She stopped by to say hi and ask what happened. A face full of ice is kind of a conversation starter. She asked how we were doing on our float research."

"Float research?" asked Kate.

"Have you already forgotten?" said Melanie. "That was our cover story at the museum."

"Oh, right. We've got so many secrets floating around, it's tough to keep them all straight. What did you tell her?"

"Well, I tried to be vague. I did say we were looking forward to the parade tomorrow, and she said she'd be there, too. She wanted to see Mr. Simmington's last floats in person."

"Oh, yeah, I forgot," said Melanie. "If he's retiring, I guess these are his last floats."

"Looks like our parents are packing up," said Faye. "We'd better go help out."

"We'll do it," said Melanie. "You sit down."

Faye tried to help anyway, but the adults shooed her away. Together, the families from their block cleaned up their surroundings. Chairs were folded, gumbo sealed up, and drinks grabbed for the ride home.

Melanie waved goodbye to her friends and was about to hop into the van when Matt came running up.

"Hey, Melanie, I caught a few of these and thought you might want them." He held out a bunch of black roses, clearly caught from the Merry Widows.

"Wow, thanks," said Melanie. She took the roses and smiled.

Matt grinned. "No big deal. Well, see you around."

"See ya."

Melanie climbed into the vehicle and leaned back into the seat. Her little sister sat beside her, drowsy from the day's activities. Lacey slowly kicked her legs against the car seat as she fought sleep.

Melanie watched the streets pass by outside the window as her mind drifted. Silently she fingered the black roses, her mind bouncing back and forth between Matt and the Mardi Gras code. She wasn't entirely sure which posed the greater mystery.

# 12

Melanie woke up slowly on Monday morning. The party the day before had been fun, but exhausting, and she had slept hard.

She lay in bed, groggy for the moment, vaguely feeling that something interesting was supposed to happen that day. Suddenly, she remembered and jumped out of bed. Today, she would gather the final clues.

Though it was a Monday, schools weren't in session. All the area schools closed for the last Monday and Tuesday of Mardi Gras so that everyone could enjoy the festivities. It was a Mobile quirk that always made her out-of-town cousins jealous, but Melanie accepted it as normal. She found it stranger that kids in other cities actually attended school on Mardi Gras.

Melanie ran out to the kitchen. Her mother was mixing up oatmeal for breakfast. Melanie sat down at the table next to her little sister. Lacey bounced up and down in her chair while pretending to read a cereal box.

"Mommy, I don't want to go to school," said Lacey.

"Good news, then," said Mrs. Smythurst, placing a bowl of oatmeal in front of each of her daughters. She ruffled Lacey's hair. "You get to stay with me today. Except…" She sat down by Melanie and spoke to her. "Except for a couple of hours around lunchtime when I need you to watch Lacey for me."

Melanie almost choked on her oatmeal. That would be during the parade!

"But, Mom, I can't. I'm going to the Queen Hera parade today, and it starts at noon."

"You're going to another parade?" her mother asked. "What has gotten in to you, Mel? Not one week ago, you were sick of Mardi Gras, and now suddenly you're going to… what is this, the fifth parade?"

"Only the fourth," said Melanie. "Please, Mom. I've just got to go."

"Melanie, I need to meet with this client today. Your father isn't off until tomorrow, and daycare's closed. That just leaves you to watch your sister."

"Please, Mom," said Melanie again. "Just this one last parade. I can't skip it."

"Why is this one so important? There'll be another parade tonight you can go to instead. I could really use your help today. And so could Lacey."

"Mom, I promise I'll stay home all night and play with Lacey. Just let me go to the parade."

Melanie's mother stared at her pleading eyes and relented.

"Oh, all right. I'll see if I can reschedule to later this afternoon."

Melanie jumped up and hugged her mom tightly from the side.

"Ok, ok," Mrs. Smythurst said, patting Melanie's arm. "Don't choke me." Melanie pulled her arms off of her mom and returned to her oatmeal, her heart slowly stopping its pounding at her near escape. She hoped that nothing else would stand in her way.

"It is so loud out here," yelled Faye.

The girls took positions for their final Mardi Gras parade. They arrived early enough to secure spots on the barricade, ensuring a good view of every float.

The crowd was extremely dense. The early morning fog had burned off to reveal a blazing blue sky, and thousands had turned out to enjoy the festivities in the beautiful weather.

Vendors marched up and down the street, rolling carts loaded down with noisemakers, glow sticks, and cotton candy for sale before the parade began. A loudspeaker blasted out the local WKGF radio station, while a group of little boys standing near Melanie each blew hard on their cheap plastic trumpets.

"Let's talk strategy," said Faye, fighting to be heard above the overall din.

"What?" yelled Kate.

"Strategy," Faye yelled back. "Kate. You run interference on beads, keeping them from knocking us in the face. Again." She rubbed her cheek, which sported a large bruise from the day before. "Me and Mel will look for letters."

"Yes, ma'am," said Kate, with a mock salute. "Nothing will get by me."

"Works for me, too," said Melanie. She shifted from foot to foot restlessly. "When is this parade going to start? I can't wait much longer." She leaned out over the barricade and peered down the street. "I don't even see police cars yet. Let's go, people!"

"You're not excited, are you, Melanie?" said Kate.

"Aren't you?" said Melanie. "We're so close!"

"Ok, you got me," said Kate with a laugh. "For real, let's start this parade."

"I hear sirens," said Faye. "It'll be any minute now."

Slowly, two police cars drove down the street. The workers sealed off the barricades so that people could no longer cross the road. Only minutes later, the theme float came rolling through.

"Countries of the World," read Kate. "Good theme."

In between looking for letters, Melanie stopped to appreciate Mr. Simmington's workmanship.

He had clearly poured his talent into the last

batch of floats that he would design. Every float seemed to be more beautiful than the one before it.

The Italian float carried a huge replica of the leaning tower of Pisa and shimmering Venetian waters dotted with gondolas.

Next came a gorgeous float covered with the Swiss Alps, its shining snowdrifts glittering in the sunlight.

The next float depicted a Brazilian jungle. Monkeys swung on vines over rivers stocked with hippos, and leopards peered out from behind massive trees.

Majestically, the floats sailed one by one down the street. Costumed riders tossed out beads, animals, snacks, and balls to the huge crowds below. Kate caught throw after throw, more than once saving Faye or Melanie from a face full of beads. And Melanie and Faye kept their eyes trained for funny letters, slowly growing their list of clues.

When the last float passed down the street thirty minutes later, Melanie, Faye, and Kate smiled at one another. Clutched in Melanie's hand was her phone, containing what they hoped were the last clues to the mysterious puzzle they had first noticed a week ago. Time to crack the code.

The girls spread out at Melanie's kitchen table. After carefully copying the final clues onto the sheet of paper, Melanie ran off two copies for Faye and Kate from her mother's home office.

Mrs. Smythurst left for her client meeting, and

Melanie settled Lacey in front of a cartoon. Now, the three girls sat in relative quiet, each girl examining her list of clues.

"I need paper," said Faye after several minutes. "Just something to write on." She turned to Melanie. "Do you have anything we could use?"

Melanie jumped up and returned moments later with three legal pads and three pens. She passed them out at the table and sat back down silently.

Faye's pen began scratching at her legal pad. Kate leaned her chair back and propped her legs up, holding her piece of paper up in the air in front of her to read. Melanie simply stared at her paper, willing the pattern to show up in front of her eyes.

Nothing happened for Melanie. No pattern jumped out at her. She only saw a collection of random letters.

"Melanie." Melanie looked down to see Lacey leaning onto her lap. "Melanie, I want you to play with me."

"Not now, Lacey. I'm trying to work."

"Mom said you'd play with me."

"No, Mom said I'd watch you. I'm busy right now. Go back to your TV show."

Lacey sighed and trudged out of the room. Melanie heard a loud crash a few minutes later, suggesting that Lacey had dumped out all of her blocks. She gritted her teeth. She'd have to clean it up before her mom came home.

Melanie stared at the letters. She remembered hearing in a spy movie one time that you needed a cipher to unlock a code. The cipher would show you what letters or numbers really stood for. Unfortunately, she was a little fuzzy on *how* a cipher actually told you that, and, besides, she didn't have one.

She began to write out the letters one at a time, transforming them one letter further into the alphabet. So, A's became B's; B's became C's, and so on. After trying this on the first set of letters, she quickly ended up with… "Gibberish," she said.

"What?" asked Kate.

"Nothing," said Melanie. She tried transforming the letters again, this time going backwards. So, A's became Z's; B's became A's, and so forth.

Nothing again.

"Melanie." Lacey was back.

"Lacey," said Melanie in exasperation. "I am trying to think here."

"But I'm bored."

"Sorry, I can't help you. I'm trying to solve a problem."

"Oh, do you have a problem?" Lacey asked. "I know what to do with that. Princess Mia taught me." She began to belt out a song.

*A problem will not scare you,*
*If you learn what to do.*
*Start at the top and take it step by step,*
*And you can solve them, too!*

Lacey took a deep breath to continue her song.

"Oh," she bellowed, "a problem will not scare you–"

"Lacey!" yelled Melanie, stopping her. "Seriously, I can't think. No more singing. Please, just go play. I don't care what you do. Just. Go. Play."

"I'm gonna tell Mom." Lacey stomped out of the room, her blond curls bouncing with each step.

"Go ahead," grumbled Melanie.

"Siblings," said Kate, while Faye smiled at Melanie sympathetically.

They settled back to work, but Melanie had difficulty concentrating. That ridiculous Princess Mia song was stuck in her head now.

She caught herself humming it once or twice before resolutely falling silent again. Still, it kept replaying in her mind.

"Start at the top, take it step by step…"

Melanie froze. Her eyes widened as she stared at the paper.

That was it. That stupid song had given her the answer.

She started at the first parade, first letter. "Start at the top." She wrote the letter on her legal pad.

She then moved on to the next parade, top letter. "Step by Step." She wrote this letter as the second letter on her legal pad. She continued this pattern, scrolling through the five parades letter by letter, going back to the first parade when she reached the last one.

Slowly, words started emerging from the lists of letters. She could hardly believe it.

"Guys," she said shakily as she wrote. "Guys,

come look at this."

"Have you found something?" asked Faye, as she and Kate hurried behind Melanie's shoulder.

"I was making it too hard," said Melanie. "It's a simple pattern that was there in front of us the whole time. It just took Lacey's goofy song to make me see it." Melanie's heart raced as she continued to work out the code.

Finally, all three girls stared at a message, a message transmitted in secret through the Mardi Gras parades to anyone with wits enough to see it.

"'Find the intertwining letters in Church Street Cemetery,'" read Faye aloud. "'Uandm. Mardi Gras Day p.m.' What's uandm?"

"*U* and *M*," said Melanie. "It means the letters. *U* and *M*."

Melanie closed her eyes to savor the truth.

"It's real," she said, almost to herself. "It's real." Her voice slowly grew louder as she opened her eyes. "We actually found a real-life, honest-to-goodness mystery, and –" she stood up suddenly, "we solved it!"

"We cracked the code," said Faye, shaking her head in disbelief.

Kate let out a whoop. "We did it!"

Melanie and Faye took up the yell with Kate. "We did it! We did it!"

They danced around the kitchen, singing the Princess Mia song and laughing.

"Wait." Melanie raced back to the table and retrieved the sheet of paper. "Let's make sure we understand all of it." She read the message out loud again.

"All we have to do," said Faye, "is go to the cemetery tomorrow – "

"Yikes," said Kate. "I am not crazy about that part. That dark float barn was already enough to almost make me pee my pants."

"It'll be during the day, though," said Melanie. "'Mardi Gras Day, p.m.' It must mean tomorrow afternoon."

"I guess," said Kate. Still, she shivered.

"So, go tomorrow afternoon," said Melanie, "and find those letters?"

"They might be tough to find," said Faye. "I bet they're hidden."

"And assuming we find them, then what?" asked Kate.

"No idea," said Melanie with a grin. "But we'll figure it out. We've come this far, right?"

"Right!" shouted Kate and Faye. They took up the Princess Mia song again and started an impromptu square dance together, while Melanie yelled for Lacey.

"Hey, Lacey," Melanie called. "Guess what? You cracked the code for me."

Faye and Kate continued their antics, but Lacey didn't reply.

"Lace?" yelled Melanie again. "Come see."

No answer.

"Be right back," said Melanie. She walked to the living room.

"Lacey, peel yourself away from TV for a sec. Come into the kitchen."

But there was no Lacey parked in front of the television. Melanie stared into an empty room.

"Lacey?" yelled Melanie. "Where are you?"

A sick feeling started rising in her stomach as she hurried from room to room, going faster the farther she ran without finding her little sister.

She burst into the kitchen a minute later. Kate and Faye stopped singing abruptly at the sight of her wild eyes.

"It's Lacey!" cried Melanie. "She's gone!"

MAGGIE M. LARCHE

# 13

"What do you mean, 'gone'?" asked Kate. "As in, she left the house?"

"As in, missing. Missing child, that kind of gone!" yelled Melanie, her voice rising hysterically.

"Don't panic," said Faye. "We'll find her."

"I've searched the house," said Melanie. "She's not here. I'm going to check the yard."

"I'll check the house again," said Kate. "Maybe she's playing hide and seek."

Melanie dashed out the back door, Faye close on her heels.

"Lacey!" Melanie yelled. "Lacey, where are you?" She quickly scanned the yard and then turned to Faye. "I don't think she's back here. Go check the tool shed and garage. I'm going to look out front."

Faye nodded, and Melanie dashed around the

side of the house. She emerged into the front yard through the gate. Her heart fell further when she still didn't see her little sister.

She ran around the front of the house, yelling Lacey's name over and over again. Tears were pricking the corners of her eyes.

She'd been so stupid. How could she have ignored Lacey?

She ran to the sidewalk and looked up the street in one direction, then the other. No sign.

The tears started flowing faster now.

Kate and Faye joined her from behind at a fast trot.

"No sign of her," said Kate.

Faye squeezed Melanie's arm. "Come on, let's keep looking."

Melanie nodded and quickly wiped her eyes.

"Ok, I'm going to grab my bike and head that way." She pointed right. "Kate, can you go the other way? And Faye, stay here in case she comes back."

Pumping her pedals furiously down the sidewalk, Melanie raced to the corner, calling Lacey's name all the while.

Where could Lacey have gone? What was Melanie going do if something happened to her?

"This is all my fault," moaned Melanie to herself. "I should have been watching her. I was so obsessed with that code."

For something that had occupied most of her waking thoughts for days now, Melanie marveled at how quickly the Mardi Gras code lost its significance.

All of Melanie's thoughts were for her sister.

She reached the end of her street, cruising past the school bus stop.

On a whim, she turned down the side street that led to Lacey's school.

"Lacey," she called repeatedly as she rode.

"Mel!"

Melanie skidded her bike to a halt and jumped off, letting the bike rattle to the ground. She'd spotted her sister, looking impossibly small on the street by herself.

Lacey was halfway down the block, walking back in the direction towards home. She held her Princess Mia doll by the hand, dragging her on the ground. Her face lit up in a bright smile when she saw her older sister.

Melanie rushed to Lacey and enfolded her in a huge hug.

"Thank God!" she cried. "You scared the ever-loving daylights out of me. Where have you been?"

"I went to school to find a friend," said Lacey.

"By yourself?" said Melanie. "You know you're not supposed to go out alone."

"I brought Mia with me," she said, with a look that clearly said, "Duh."

"That doesn't count, Lace," said Melanie.

Lacey ignored her. "No one was at school. So I came home."

Melanie hugged Lacey again.

"Mel, why are you crying?"

"Because I thought I'd lost you, you little

maniac." She stood up and wiped her face once more. Then she grabbed Lacey's hand. "Come on," she said, shaking her head. "Let's go home."

She retrieved her bike and walked it back with Lacey by her side. She'd run out of the house without her phone, so she couldn't call Kate or Faye to let them know of Lacey's safety. They advanced slowly, moving at a three-year-old's pace, but Melanie was much too relieved to care. Slowly, her heart returned to a normal beat.

A few minutes later, she heard Kate's voice calling, "Lacey."

"Kate," yelled Melanie. "It's ok. I've got her."

Kate popped around the corner on her bicycle. "Whew! That's a relief." She smiled at Lacey. "Good to see you, kiddo. Where were you?"

Melanie said, "She tried to go to school. She walked all the way down the block."

"What?" exclaimed Kate.

"I just wanted someone to play with me," said Lacey. "Melanie was busy."

Kate glanced at Melanie. "She really knows how to guilt a person, huh?"

Melanie nodded.

Kate turned her bike around. "Well, I'll go let Faye know we've got her. See you back at your house."

Melanie and Lacey continued their slow trek.

"Are you done working, now?" asked Lacey suddenly.

Melanie thought back to the code they'd solved.

She couldn't really believe that she and her friends had been celebrating in the kitchen scarcely half an hour ago. Melanie felt as if she'd aged at least a year in that short time.

"Yeah, Bug. I'm done working now. Thanks to you. Did you know that you helped us solve the puzzle?"

"I did?" cried Lacey.

"You did," said Melanie. "And since you helped, you're a part of the group now. Tomorrow, we find out what it all means, and we couldn't have done it without you."

Kate and Faye left soon after Melanie and Lacey arrived back home.

"I can only take so much excitement," said Faye. She gave Lacey a quick hug. "I'm glad you're back."

The three friends said goodbye.

"Tomorrow," said Kate, uncharacteristically solemn.

"Tomorrow," said Melanie.

"Tomorrow," said Faye.

Melanie spent the rest of the afternoon playing games and puzzles with Lacey, even after her mother returned from the client meeting. Losing her sister for that brief time had been a bigger emotional shock than Melanie wanted to admit, and she was happy to curl up with Lacey on the couch for hours. And though Mrs. Smythurst may have found this strange, she never did find out the reason why.

Going to bed that evening, Melanie's head felt

clear and ready for the next day's adventure. After all they had accomplished, she was sure that she and her friends could find the intertwining $U$ and $M$ in the graveyard. The question of what those clues would lead to, however, haunted her thoughts, and long after she lay down to sleep, she was tantalized by shadowy visions of mysteries revealed.

# 14

Fat Tuesday dawned cool and bright. Melanie spent the slow morning lounging in her pajamas and watching TV. With her entire family off for the day, it felt like a Saturday. After a late family brunch, Melanie finally headed back to her room to get ready for her afternoon adventure.

Melanie dressed with special attention that day. Though she didn't know exactly what awaited her in the cemetery, she felt that it would be momentous. She carefully selected her clothing, feeling as if she were a priestess preparing for an ancient ritual. Today, she was no ordinary twelve-year-old girl. She was Melanie Smythurst, heroine.

Lacey sat on Melanie's bed and watched her get dressed. Even she seemed to sense the importance of the occasion, for she sat relatively still and quiet next to the row of stuffed animals she brought to observe the proceedings.

After the previous day's fiasco, Melanie didn't mind Lacey's presence as much as she might have normally. She even let Lacey pick out one of her headbands to borrow.

Finally, shoes on and ponytail in place, Melanie was ready.

Lacey fussed momentarily when she realized Melanie would be leaving her. She jumped off the bed.

"No, don't go. Let's play together today."

Melanie knelt down in front of her younger sister. She placed her hands on either of Lacey's arms and looked at her seriously.

"Remember you helped us solve the riddle yesterday. Right?"

Lacey nodded.

"Well, I've got to go finish it now. Since you helped us, you're in on the secret, but we have to do this part by ourselves. You be a big girl for Mom and Dad, and I'll tell you all about it when I get back."

"Promise?"

"Promise."

"Oh, ok. But I'll miss you."

Melanie stood up.

"Remember, it's our secret. No telling Mom and Dad."

Lacey nodded, and Melanie walked her out the door of her room.

The night before, Melanie had painstakingly

mapped out the best path to the cemetery and asked that everyone meet at noon on the street. Melanie chose the time carefully. It could be tricky travelling around town on Fat Tuesday, as parades and barricades could send you on a detour without warning. By leaving at noon, Melanie hoped they would make it to the parade route just after the midday parade ended. She expected the crowds to be a little lighter as everyone went off to find lunch.

She was right. As the girls bicycled through the streets, they made their way easily towards the cemetery. With every block they covered, Melanie felt the excitement rising like a tide that carried all three of them along with it. Finally, she rode the thrill like the crest of a wave, glimpsing the gates of the cemetery up ahead.

Church Street Cemetery housed some of the oldest graves in the city. Stuck right in the middle of downtown, the graveyard was a quiet oasis surrounded by a low brick wall that encircled the entire three acres of land.

The girls stood under the arched entryway and surveyed the cemetery.

Kate read the sign on the gate. "'Established 1819 by City of Mobile for yellow fever victims.' Oh yeah, not creepy at all."

Melanie heard the hubbub of the crowd a block away. Strains of jazz music floated on the air behind them. In front of them, all was silent.

"Well, here goes," said Kate. Faye took a deep breath, and Melanie crossed herself. Then they walked through and into the quiet.

"Remember, we've got to find an intertwining *U* and *M*," said Melanie, feeling as though she should speak quietly. "Should we split up? It'll make it go faster."

"No way," said Faye. "I have seen too many horror movies to split up in a graveyard. I say we stay together."

"Ditto," said Kate.

Melanie didn't say so aloud, but she was glad. After the noise of the Mardi Gras madness behind them, the cemetery seemed much too quiet. Eerily quiet.

"Then let's get started," said Melanie. "We'll need to check all the gravestones, and anything else in here. Look for trees with carvings, graffiti on the outside wall, anything. Intertwining *U* and *M*."

Kate and Faye nodded, and the three friends started down the first path to their right. Their footsteps made no noise on the cushioned grass.

The gravestones were all old and darkened with age. Melanie found three in a row that dated from the early 1800s. She checked every stone she passed. Though many were covered with very ornate writing, she didn't see anything that would qualify as an intertwined set of the correct letters.

Many of the graves lay flat against the ground, but some rose up as full tombs, ranging from a few inches off the ground to about eight feet high.

There were gates within the larger gate as well, surrounding smaller groupings of gravesites, which the girls had to wind through. Melanie put Faye in charge of keeping track of which rows they'd checked so they didn't get confused with all the snaking back and forth.

After fifteen minutes, Kate called out, "I've found something."

As Melanie and Faye rushed to her side, Kate hurried to clarify. "Not the *U* and *M*. Sorry. But I found Joe Cain's grave."

A long stone tablet marked the grave.

"Here lies Old Joe Cain," read Melanie. "The heart and soul of Mardi Gras in Mobile." The face of a reveler was engraved beside the inscription.

Faye pointed out a black silk rose lying on the tombstone beside a pile of black beads. "It looks like Joe Cain's widows have already been here." She reached down and picked up the flower and tucked it in her hair.

"Beautiful," said Kate. "Let me have the beads. I'll split them with you, Mel."

But Melanie wasn't paying attention. Her eyes were transfixed on the tombstone. Unknowingly, Faye had revealed a small symbol hidden beneath the black rose.

Two capital letters, a *U* with an *M* on top of it. The bottom of the two legs of the *M* wrapped around the sides of the *U*.

"Intertwining *U* and *M*," breathed Melanie.

Wordlessly, she gripped the arms of her friends. They stopped talking and followed Melanie's eyes downward. They drew in their breath sharply at the same time.

Kate dropped to her knees to examine the symbol more closely.

"There's something else here," she said.

The other girls joined her on the ground.

"What is that?" asked Faye. "It's so faint."

"Looks like an arrow," said Melanie. "But what's it pointing to?" She turned in the direction of the arrow's head.

The girls were standing near the edge of the cemetery. Following the arrow, all that lay between Joe Cain's grave and the outer wall were a few small gravestones and one large tomb.

Slowly, Melanie walked in that direction. She couldn't see anything noteworthy. She examined each of the gravestones closely and walked along the inside of the brick wall. Nothing.

Finally, she advanced to the tomb. She didn't notice anything out of place at first and began to turn away again. Then her eyes caught a very small engraving by the door handle.

"Guys. I know what it's telling us." Melanie looked at the tomb door.

Faye stared at her in horror, while Kate looked confused.

"What?" asked Kate, glancing back and forth between her two friends. "What's it telling us?" Suddenly she paused, and comprehension dawned on her face.

"You have *got* to be kidding me. You're saying we have to go in there?"

Melanie nodded.

"Into a grave?"

"Technically, it's a tomb," said Faye.

"Oh, that's much better."

The three friends gathered in front of the stone building. It was one of the larger structures in the cemetery, about the size of a small garden shed. Melanie guessed that the ceiling would be a few feet above their heads, assuming they ever went inside.

The door to the tomb was almost devoid of markings. Besides the small symbol that matched the one on Joe Cain's grave, the girls saw only a single inscription: "Julius and Emily Malthus. Underground, but above."

"I wonder what's in there," said Faye.

"Besides old Mr. and Mrs. Malthus," said Kate.

Melanie groaned. "So now what?"

"Can we really go in?" asked Faye. "Should we? It seems wrong."

All three girls stared at the door as if it would somehow answer Faye's question.

"We broke into a float barn," said Faye.

"Matt was arrested," said Kate.

"We practically lost my sister," said Melanie.

A heavy silence.

"Let's do it," said Faye.

As one, they nodded, and Melanie reached out to turn the handle.

Slowly, the heavy metal door swung open. It made no noise, as if it were kept greased and well maintained. The girls found themselves looking into the inside of an honest-to-goodness tomb.

Melanie forced down the fear in her throat and looked inside.

She found herself staring at the back of a dark figure.

Next to Melanie, Kate sounded as though she were about to hyperventilate, and Faye clutched Melanie's arm tightly. Melanie herself cringed as the mysterious apparition slowly turned to face them.

This is it, thought Melanie. We're going to die. We're going to die at the hands of a ghost on Mardi Gras day.

# 15

The ghost turned to face them. To Melanie's surprise, he had an enormous grin on his face.

"Welcome!" he said. "I wasn't sure if anyone would be coming this year."

The girls stared at him.

"Are you dead?" asked Kate.

The man laughed and stepped closer to the door. The girls instinctively shrank back.

As he entered the light, though, they realized a couple of facts. First, he was not a ghost; he appeared to be an elderly man dressed in a warm sweater and corduroys. Second, he looked absolutely delighted to see them.

"I'm sorry," he said, continuing to chuckle. "I didn't intend to frighten you, though I see now that's exactly what I did. Still," he winked, "the element of mystery is part of the fun, right?"

Melanie closed her mouth which had fallen open. "I'm sorry – what?"

"You clearly don't realize it, but you've just found the headquarters of Mobile's most secret society. We are the Underground Mystics."

He stepped to the side and held his arm out with a flourish.

"Please come inside and take a look."

The girls exchanged uncertain glances before Melanie and Faye stepped carefully into the room. Kate resolutely stood outside. Though she didn't say so in so many words, Melanie knew Kate wasn't about to let all three of them get locked into a tomb by a crazy person. Which was fair, as far as Melanie was concerned.

But Melanie couldn't stay back. Her curiosity was too strong.

As she stepped into the dark tomb, it took a moment for her eyes to adjust to the dim light. A camp lantern lit up the interior, but the darkness still contrasted sharply with the bright daylight outside.

She was relieved to see that this was one tomb that held no dead bodies, in spite of the inscription on the door. Even her burning desire to solve the mystery probably wouldn't hold up against meeting actual corpses.

Instead, the tomb was a small, rectangular room with stone walls. On the wall to her left, a purple banner stretched across the stone.

"Underground Mystics," read Melanie.

Underneath the banner were two long scrolls. The first was considerably yellowed with age; the second, only slightly less so. Each scroll listed line after line of small script. On the wall ahead of her hung a framed black and white picture of an elderly couple. The final wall displayed several newspaper clippings preserved in heavy frames. In one corner sat a small folding chair and a mystery novel that the old man appeared to have been reading to pass the time.

Melanie turned to the man.

"Who are you?"

"Oh, I am sorry," he said. "My manners have lapsed. My name is Mr. Simmington. And you are?"

"You're Mr. Simmington?" Melanie cried. "The float designer?"

Mr. Simmington nodded modestly. "Yes, how gratifying to know you have heard of me. I have indeed designed many floats in my time. Though now I would have to say that I am Mr. Simmington, the *retired* float designer."

Kate, who had obviously been listening outside, stuck her head around the door. "You're Mr. Simmington? I called you on the phone." She walked inside the tomb. "You wouldn't talk to me."

"Ah," he said. "You were the 'school project' call?"

Kate nodded.

"I'm sorry," said Mr. Simmington again. "That was rude of me, but you see, I try to keep a low profile. It makes my work for the Underground

Mystics that much more satisfying. You'll have to pardon me."

"The Underground Mystics," repeated Melanie. "Who are they?"

"We, my dear, are an exclusive group of individuals who have solved the initiation riddle. No one joins the Underground Mystics without first earning it. No easy sign-up and paying dues for us. No, every member of the Undergrounds, as we call ourselves, found their way here by their own wits and ingenuity."

He settled down into his chair.

"Do you ladies mind if I sit? I'm not the young man I once was."

"Sure," said Faye.

"How do people find their way in?" asked Melanie.

"Well, presumably the way you three did," he said. "I assume you found your way here after decoding the message I placed in this year's parades?"

"Yes," said Melanie, smiling for the first time since this strange episode had begun. "We first saw the letters in the Centaurs parade, and then followed the rest of the code from there."

"There you are then," said Mr. Simmington. "You see, every year, the Undergrounds place a new secret message into Mardi Gras. Sometimes it's a message hidden between the music of the marching bands. Other times we send out secret emissaries at the balls. One year we even sewed our coded invitation into the Merry Widows' black veils." He smiled reminiscently. "That was a fine one. And quite difficult to achieve without the Widows realizing what we were up to.

"As this was my last year actively designing floats, I thought I'd have one last hurrah and hide the secret in the floats themselves." He smiled brightly. "And I'm so glad that someone discovered my invitation." He gestured around the room. "Please feel free to look around."

The girls slowly circled the small room. They examined the scroll up close and saw a list of names. The girls scanned the recent additions.

"Hey," said Kate, "isn't that the mayor?"

"Look," said Faye. "Sasha Tipton's on here!"

"Oh, do you know Sasha? She's a sweet girl and very clever. She helped me plan out the code this year. The code itself is fairly simple to come up with, but inserting it into the floats without too many people noticing can be tricky."

"All that time," said Kate, "and we could have asked her for help."

"I'm glad we didn't," said Melanie, and Mr. Simmington nodded in approval.

She circled to the picture on the wall. It showed an elderly couple in black and white leaning back against an old automobile. The photograph looked like it had been well cared for over the years.

"Who are they?" she asked.

"Ah," said Mr. Simmington, "those are our founders, Julius and Emily Malthus. Perhaps you noticed their names on the door?"

The girls nodded.

"We thought they might be in here," said Kate.

Mr. Simmington laughed. "Well, I'd be lying if I said that wasn't the general impression we like to give." He examined the girls. "As you've come all this way, would you like to hear their story?"

"Yes," said Melanie, surprised at the eagerness in her own voice.

Mr. Simmington leaned back and crossed one leg on top of the other.

"Julius and Emily Malthus were a very wealthy couple. Big fixtures in the Mobile old money scene. But, being both quite intelligent, they got a little bored with the usual society events.

"As the story goes, they were sitting together one evening after one such event, and Mrs. Malthus was complaining of the boring party from which they had just returned. She challenged her husband to gather together people who were a little more interesting. A little more clever. All around, a little more Emily Malthus's style.

"Well, being a sporting man, Mr. Malthus immediately took up the challenge.

"He reasoned that finding a group of sharp thinking people meant that those people would somehow have to prove that they were, in fact, clever. So he came up with the idea of sending out an encrypted invitation that encouraged those who solved it to join together for mutual benefit and entertainment.

"The particular method Mr. Julius selected was a series of coded messages through the newspaper want ads. I doubt you young ladies read newspapers nowadays, but in the 1910s, they were the lifeblood of the community." He gestured to the wall behind him. "These are his ads, here. By some stroke of prescience, his wife saved them, and we are able to preserve them as part of our group heritage.

"So he sent out a coded invitation for any who wished to join him and his wife at his home at a certain day and hour. They were instructed to tell no one of where they were going.

"In all, five guests showed up at that first meeting. One was a prominent local doctor. One a young housewife. Two were teachers at a local college. And one was a dockworker in the city's port.

"It was an unusual gathering, as you might expect, but it was also a delightful one. Mrs. Malthus was so pleased with her husband's ingenuity, and with the results, that she suggested they find a way to continue the practice.

"Thus, the idea of the Underground Mystics was born. They conceived the plan of somehow connecting the group with Mardi Gras, to stay true to Mobile's culture, while still maintaining complete secrecy. And the very next Mardi Gras season, the next invitation was issued. Four more people joined as a result.

"After a couple more years, Mr. Malthus had the idea to convert this tomb to the headquarters, so to speak. It was originally going to be for his and his bride's use in the hereafter, but I rather fancy they liked the mysterious quality of putting group headquarters in a graveyard. Mr. Malthus had a flair for the dramatic. The tomb has never been a gathering place, obviously – it's too small for that – but it is a place to preserve our heritage.

"And so it has continued to this day."

"Wow," said Faye. "That is amazing."

"Really cool," said Kate.

"So," said Melanie, "the Undergrounds are really a secret society?"

Mr. Simmington nodded. "Oh yes, the most secret in Mobile. At least," he winked, "to my knowledge. You see, many other groups hide their membership. After all, that's part of the appeal of Mardi Gras. As my late wife used to say, you'd be surprised what you can do when you're wearing a mask.

"But the Undergrounds are different. While the other groups hide their membership, we hide our existence. We exist for ourselves only. Even after 100 years, our organization continues to be the best kept secret in town."

"But if you're such a secret, what do you guys do?" asked Kate. "Throw secret parties?"

Mr. Simmington smiled. "By some standards, we don't really do much at all. We don't parade. We don't show off at balls and at society events. And we don't even all know each other. But, we've all got this one common bond – we faced an intriguing problem and, instead of ignoring it, of going on to other things, we decided to tackle it. To solve the puzzle, break the code, uncover the mystery. It's a bond of initiative and of imagination.

"And that, ladies, can be more fun than all the balls, parades, and feasting in the world. That is what the Underground Mystics are all about."

Melanie grinned. "And we found you." She turned to Faye and Kate and saw her own pride mirrored in her friend's faces.

"Yes, you did," said Mr. Simmington, "But, my dear girls, I don't think you quite understand. You haven't just found us. You've earned the right to join us, if you so wish."

Melanie stared at him in surprise.

"Really?" asked Kate.

"Us?" said Faye.

"Of course."

Melanie caught her breath. The conversation of the last few minutes had proceeded so quickly that her head felt a little wonky. Did she want to join this group?

"Yes," she thought almost immediately. After all, wasn't this exactly what she'd been looking for the last couple of weeks? She'd followed the steps, chasing the hope that maybe everyday could hide a little more mystery than what she saw daily. And here she'd found a gathering of people who'd all followed that same hope in their own lives.

But even as she recognized her willingness to join, she felt a heavy weight settle in her stomach. She realized that she should first let Mr. Simmington know something – their ages. He might not realize just how young they actually were, and the Undergrounds might not want kids in their group.

Reluctantly, she spoke. "Mr. Simmington, you should probably know that we're only twelve years old."

"Thank you for informing me of that fact," he said solemnly, "but I have only to reply: What of it? Ingenuity knows no age. In fact, you younger folks are probably better endowed with it than most of our older membership."

Melanie immediately felt lighter. She looked at her friends with a question on her face. Faye gave a small nod and smile, and Kate said, "Let's do it."

"Mr. Simmington, thank you," said Melanie. "We would love to join."

"Excellent," he said, standing up slowly from the chair. "Then we have two points of order to accomplish. First, you will take an oath of secrecy. And second, you shall sign our scroll of membership."

He crossed to the small table inside the door and picked up the small leather-bound notebook. He opened it, and it cracked with age.

"Very well, please all face me." The three girls lined up side by side. "Now, repeat after me.

"I hereby join the Underground Mystics."

The girls dutifully repeated his words as he continued the oath.

"As keepers of the tradition, I will tell of our elite organization to no one. I will guard both the secret of our group and the spark of creativity and curiosity which led me here."

He closed the book and beamed at Melanie and her friends. "Welcome to the Undergrounds."

The girls grinned.

"Now, you get to sign the scroll." He pointed to the second of the long papers pinned to the wall and handed them a pen from the table.

Kate took the pen first and signed her name with a flourish. Faye went next and carefully added her name underneath Kate's. She passed the pen to Melanie.

Melanie stepped up to the scroll.

"Mr. Simmington, we actually have a fourth member of our group who helped solve the code. She couldn't come with us today, but she earned the right as much as we did. May I add her?"

"If she helped solve the mystery, then she has certainly earned her membership as well. Can she be entrusted with this secret, do you think?"

"I do."

"Then, sign away," he said. "Bring her by next year, and she can take the official oath as well."

Melanie grinned as she pictured Lacey in this room, taking the solemn oath in her slight lisp. It would be a sight to look forward to over the coming year.

Melanie signed her own name first, using cursive to make it more official. All her work had been for this moment, and she felt the pride of it deep in her heart.

"You know," Mr. Simmington said to Kate and Faye, "I'd wager that you three are the youngest members in our organization's history. It's difficult to know for certain, of course, but I don't doubt it."

Melanie smiled as she slowly wrote the name "Lacey Smythurst" on the scroll.

"I'm willing to bet," she murmured, "that our fourth member will take the youngest prize."

As Mr. Simmington didn't see anyone else nosing around the cemetery looking for clues, he briefly left his post to walk the girls back to the main parade route.

"Some years we get several people; some years none," he said. "It varies."

The girls pushed their bikes at a leisurely pace to match Mr. Simmington's speed. As they walked, he made them recount how they discovered and deciphered the code. He nodded approvingly when Melanie described the orderly step-by-step approach they had followed and laughed uproariously when Faye reluctantly shared the story of how they had snuck into the float barn. When he heard how Lacey had helped them find the correct order of the letters, he smiled and said he was pleased that Lacey would be in the Undergrounds as well.

When they reached the corner where they would part, he solemnly shook each of their hands.

"Thank you, ladies. It's been lovely meeting you, and I do hope you'll call on me if you ever need anything.

"And next year about this time," he said, his eye

twinkling, "keep a look out for any messages from the Underground. You may eventually be called upon to create a new round of clues."

The girls wished him goodbye and thanked him. Then they mounted their bikes and set off for home.

Twenty minutes later, the girls coasted to a stop in front of Faye's house. They lingered on their bikes, none of them wanting the magical afternoon to end just yet.

"I wish we could tell people," said Kate.

"Me, too," said Faye.

"Do you know," said Melanie, "I don't really mind keeping it a secret."

"I knew you wouldn't," said Faye, smiling.

"So now what?" asked Kate.

"I don't know," said Melanie. "Go back to business as usual?" But deep inside, she couldn't. She might still experience times of boredom and routine, but she didn't feel she'd ever go completely back to where she had been a week ago.

"Well, I know what I'm going to do," said Kate. "I am going to take a long bubble bath and hog the bathroom for hours. Then I'm going to talk Mom into a girl's movie tonight. Get a break from the boys and unwind."

"Ooh, good plan," said Melanie.

"And when we get back," Kate continued, "I guess I'll have a little talk with Matt."

Melanie froze, waiting for the rest of the thought.

"He's a good brother – most of the time," continued Kate, "and you're a good friend, and... well, why shouldn't the two of you hang out, if you want to?"

Melanie grinned. "You sure you don't mind?"

"Nah."

Melanie gave Kate a tight hug.

"Thanks, *Katie*."

"Not funny."

The girls all giggled.

"I'm so glad that's taken care of," said Faye, smiling. "You know, I was thinking I might volunteer at the Mardi Gras museum with Sasha."

"I thought you were already stressed out with too much to do," said Kate.

"I was. But I'm bound to have a little free time now, because I am dropping that stupid violin." Kate and Melanie laughed.

"What are you going to do?" Faye asked Melanie.

Melanie stayed quiet for a second. "I think," she said, "that I am first going to go inside and tell Lacey the news. Then, I am going to sit down and write up this whole crazy adventure. I don't want us to forget a thing."

She smiled. "And who knows? I might even give it to the Undergrounds one day. Maybe it can go up on the wall, too."

The three girls parted with plans to meet the next morning at the bus stop, knowing that by the time they met, the sun would have set on another unforgettable Mardi Gras season.

# TELL ME WHAT
# YOU THINK!

Did you enjoy this heartwarming mystery? Then please go with a parent to Amazon.com and leave a review!

Reviews help other kids know which books to try. Tell the world why you liked *The Mardi Gras Chase* and earn a BIG thank you from Maggie M. Larche!

# WANT TO GET

# A FREE BOOK?

Then go with a parent to www.maggiemlarche.com and sign up for my newsletter. You'll get a free download of one of my newest books just for signing up!

Then, I'll let you know in the future about any new books coming out. It's a double-win!

# ABOUT THE AUTHOR

Maggie M. Larche loves to sing, read, and swing right alongside her kids. All of her stories feature courageous, smart, funny kids, because that's who her readers are!

She is the author of the award-winning *Striker Jones* series, a groundbreaking approach to teach economics to children through mystery stories. She lives on the beautiful Gulf Coast with her family.

# TRUE GIRLS SERIES

The Mardi Gras Chase is the first of the True Girls series, stories of girls with heart and intelligence, with just a touch of romance!

~A sneak peak at the next True Girls ~

Look for more True Girls stories coming soon! In the meantime, take a look at some other books by the author.

# OTHER SERIES BY MAGGIE M. LARCHE

## Striker Jones Series

Fans of Encyclopedia Brown will love Striker Jones, classic kids detective stories with an economics twist! Can you solve the mystery with Striker?

## Charlie Bingham

Featherbrained, lovable Charlie Bingham is always getting into scrapes. These hilarious stories will keep you laughing while Charlie finds his way out of trouble – again!

# Find them all on Amazon!

28822925R00084

Made in the USA
Middletown, DE
03 February 2016